I JUST WANNA CUFF YOU

LAYLA & SHON'S STORY WRITTEN BY: NIKKI NICOLE

D1359532

Copyright © 2018 by Nikki Nicole

Published by Pushing Pen Presents

All rights reserved.

www.authoressnikkinicole.com

This book or any portion thereof may not be reproduced or used in any manner whatsoever without the express written permission of the publisher except for the use of brief quotations in a book review.

All rights reserved. This book or any portion thereof may not be reproduced or used in any manner whatsoever without the express written permission of the publisher except for the use of brief quotations in a book review.

This book is a work of fiction. Names, characters, places, and incidents either are the product of the author's imagination or are used fictitiously and are not to be considered as real. Any resemblance, events, or locales or, is entirely coincidental.

Acknowledgments

Hi, how are you? I'm Nikki Nicole the Pen Goddess. Each time I complete a book I love to write acknowledgements. I love to give a reflection on how I felt about the book. I've been writing for two years now and this is my 16th book. When I first started writing I only had one story I wanted to tell and that was Baby I Play for Keeps. Two years later and I've penned a total of 16 books. I appreciate each one of you for taking this journey with me. I'm forever grateful for you believing in me and giving me your continuous support.

Book 16 is special to me because I'm closing something special. I swear I'm in love with this book. I love Sphinx, Shon and Vell. I love them so much. All three of them are special to me. I've spent so much time with them these past few weeks I'm not ready to let them go. Leah and Layla drove me fuckin' crazy and Malone got on my last damn nerves. It's so much growth in this book it's ridiculous. I didn't even know how I was going to finish the book, but somehow, I made it happen.

I wanted to write about love and passion. People change and deserve second chances and I wanted to showcase that. Some people are so quick to give up and walk away it's crazy. We're all human and we all make mistakes but it's up to you to learn from them.

I dedicate this book to my Queens in the Trap. I swear y'all are the best. Y'all go so hard in the paint for me it's insane. Every day we lit. I appreciate y'all more than y'all will ever know. The Trap is going up on a Tuesday. I can't wait for y'all to read it.

It's time for my S/O **Samantha, Tatina, Asha, Shanden (PinkDiva), Padrica, Liza, Aingsley Trecie, Quack, Shemekia, Toni, Amisha, Tamika, Troy, Pat, Crystal C, Missy, Angela, Latoya, Helene, Tiffany, Lamaka, Reneshia, Charmaine, Misty, Toy, Toi, Shelby, Chanta, Jessica, Snowie, Jessica, Sommer, Cathy, Karen, Bria, Kelis, Lisa, Tina, Talisha, Naquisha, Iris, Nicole, Koi, Drea, Rickena, Saderia, Chanae, Shanise, Nacresha, Jalisa, Tamika H, Kendra, Meechie, Avis, Lynette, Pamela, Antoinette, Crystal W, Ivee, Kimberly, Yutanzia, Seanise, Chrishae, Demetria, Jennifer, Shatavia, LaTonya, Dimitra, Kellissa, Jawanda, Renea,**

Tomeika, Viola, Gigi, Barbie, Erica, Shanequa, Dallas, Verona, Catherine

If I named everybody, I will be here all day. Put your name here_____ if I missed you. The list goes on. S/O to every member in my reading group, I love y'all to the moon and back. These ladies right here are a hot mess. I love them to death. They go so hard about these books it doesn't make any sense. Sometimes, I feel like I should run and hide.

If you're looking for us meet us in **Nikki Nicole's Readers Trap** on Facebook, we are live and indirect all day.

S/O to My Pen Bae's **Ash ley, Chyna L, Chiquita, T. Miles,** I love them to the moon and back head over to Amazon and grab a book by them also.

To my new readers I have five complete series, and three completed standalones available.

Cuffed by a Trap God 1-3

I Just Wanna Cuff You (Standalone)

Baby I Play for Keeps 1-3

For My Savage, I Will Ride or Die

He's My Savage, I'm His Ridah

You Don't Miss A Good Thing, Until It's Gone (Standalone)

He's My Savage, I'm His Ridah

Journee & Juelz 1-3

Giselle & Dro (Standalone)

Our Love Is the Hoodest 1-2

Join my readers group **Nikki Nicole's Readers Trap** on **Facebook**

Follow me on Facebook Nikki Taylor

Follow me on Twitter @WatchNikkiwrite

Like my Facebook Page AuthoressNikkiNicole

Instagram @WatchNikkiwrite

GoodReads @authoressnikkinicole

Visit me on the web authoressnikkinicole.com

email me authoressnikkinicole@gmail.com

Join my email contact list for exclusive sneak peaks.
http://eepurl.com/czCbKL

Table of Contents

BE CAREFUL WITH ME ...

PROLOGUE
EIGHT
MONTHS AGO

Chapter-1

Layla

Sphinx opened up some old wounds asking me about Malone and Shon. I loved Shon with everything in me. Damn, I loved him more than I loved myself. How is that even fuckin' possible? It was my reality. I lost myself behind him. I was so young, dumb and naïve back then. He was everything to me, but he didn't want to do right by me. Why didn't Shon want to do right by me? I always wanted to know that. I guess somethings are better left unsaid. I always second guessed myself when it came to us. We were together for ten years. I'm thirty-two now. I gave him all my teenage years and most of my twenties. If somebody would have told me that Shon and I wouldn't be together I wouldn't have believed them. That was a fact and a given because it was real.

Shon was my first everything. I was a fool in love for him. He had me so wide open. His cologne was the only scent I wanted to smell and inhale. His touch turned me on in the worst way. In his arms was the only place I wanted to be. He was the only oxygen that I wanted to breathe. Shon was the type of man my mother should've warned me about. Back then I wasn't trying to hear it. I Ignored all the signs and went with the flow. I decided to try love. I don't regret it, I just learned some valuable lessons along the way.

I trusted him with my life and he cheated on me. He was a hustler, his daddy was a hustler and his momma was, too. Lonnie was different though. She was an angel. She didn't get that hustle gene. She hustled books and dolls. That's what the fuck I should've done instead of riding shot gun with him. I couldn't shake him, I only wanted him. I started dating Shon when I was fifteen. We went to school together.

I remember when I first met him. I remember that day like it was yesterday. I didn't have many girlfriends, so I would always walk home by myself. It was Wednesday, February 12th to be exact. When I got off Bus 200 Shon, Dino, and Twin got off too.

It wasn't many people that rode my bus, so I knew something was up because they didn't live over here. I could feel it. Shon never said anything to me in school. I walked ahead of them because the last thing I needed was for somebody to tell my brother they saw me walking with three boys. Shon ran up on me and I dropped my books. I was pissed off because if he wanted to get my attention, he should've just called my name.

I jumped immediately, and Shon started laughing. He helped me with my books and asked me for my phone number. I was a little shy because my brother Vell was so fuckin' crazy and he was always running off boys that tried to talk to me. I gave it to him and we started talking for a few weeks. My metro phone was booming. He finally asked me to be his girlfriend and I said yes. Shon and I were connected at the hip. Whenever you saw him you saw me.

I used to sneak out of the house to be with him. I watched that niggas back like it was my own when he was heavy in the streets trapping. I was always trained to go because of who my brother was. I had to be prepared at any given time. Shon taught me how to apply pressure. I was his muscle when Dino and Twin weren't around. If he told me to shoot, I let that bitch rip until it wasn't any more bullets in the clip. If he wanted me to drive, then I could take control of the steering wheel.

I caught my first body at the age of seventeen. A nigga tried to rob him and caught him off guard because he wasn't paying attention. Shon and I will take that shit to the grave with us. The niggas that sent him, Shon and I rode up on their pussy ass'. I wasn't going out like that. Shon was my heart and I wasn't prepared to lose him ever. He was my Clyde and I was his Bonnie. Every hoe on the Eastside wanted Shon but I had HIM. I had all of him. If he was cheating, I didn't know about it, unless a chick made it known. What Shon and I had was different, so I thought. I thought we really had something special.

Shon started making major moves. He had met a connect from Cuba. San Juan was his name. When Shon and San Juan started doing business together, the money was coming in so fuckin' fast that I had to count that shit twice. We had bank rolls that wouldn't fuckin' fold.

We were up suddenly. Shon brought us a nice three-story home in Alpharetta. It was big and beautiful, and I called it the Glass House. He cashed the fuck out. You couldn't tell me shit when Shon brought us that house. Everything was brand new.

I ran up a check in Rooms to Go. Our house was laid. As soon as we moved in together shit started to change for the worse. I stopped trapping with him because he didn't want me in the streets anymore. He started hanging out all night and not coming home. I wasn't having that shit. I was doing all kind of pop ups. I was home alone all the time.

I was sick of it. He gave me money to pacify my feelings and brought me anything and everything that I wanted, but that didn't suffice. I wasn't with Shon for the material things.

I was with him when he didn't have it like that. I wasn't like the other women that wanted him for his money. Shon and my brother taught me how to get a bag. I could go out and get my own with or without him.

Shon got reckless with his shit. Females were playing on my phone left and right. He brought me a C-Class Benz. I swear my tires would magically be flat or my car would be keyed. I didn't bother anybody, so I knew it had to be a bitch he was entertaining, but I needed proof. I couldn't confront Shon until I got it.

Baby when I say the proof came in the flesh a few weeks later. I would never forget that night Shon and I was having dinner at Houston's. A bitch approached our table and grabbed a seat. She was a bold bitch. I'll never forget that bitch for as long as I live. I love bold bitches because I can't wait to tame a bold bitch. Her name was Sidney and I'm sure SHE'LL never forget how I TAPPED that ASS.

I'm sitting here waiting on Shon to check this bitch like he was supposed to. I'm fuming hot, if you don't do shit you gone fuckin' respect me or I'm taking it. He never did it, so I had too because he wasn't about to disrespect me, and she wasn't either.

I politely stood to my feet and he gazed up at me. Now was the time he should've checked that hoe the moment that bitch sat down. I know she didn't know me, but she knew of me. She for damn sure didn't want to get introduced. I never bothered anybody. I always waited on a bitch to make the first move. When she sat down at the table, that was her move.

Shon forgot how fuckin' quick I'll pop off and turn up in any motherfuckin' crowd. I didn't give a fuck about us being in Houston's.

Wherever a bitch had the balls to try me at, was the exact same place they were going to get it at. It ain't no waiting until I catch you again. I'll catch you today since you're making your presence known. I'm Haitian and I don't give a fuck. I'll get shit cracking anywhere. I asked this bitch what her problem and issue was. Everything was a joke to her. I got something for silly bitches. She was a cocky bitch too but not cockier than me.

This bitch had the nerve to say that she was fucking him all bad and nonchalant. Why the fuck did she say that? He didn't say shit. He just he his head down in his hands. He knew he fucked up.

I walked over to him and slapped the shit out of his ass. I grabbed a glass of wine and threw it in his face. Everybody was looking.

Don't ever disrespect me or play me like a fool. Shaolin Baptiste didn't raise nann fuckin' fool. The bitch was still laughing. She thought this shit was a game. Our table was setup real pretty. Too bad this bitch was about to eat every fuckin' dish on this table. I grabbed a knife and fork. The plates were already laid out for us. I smashed a plate in this bitch face. I made her eat every fucking laugh she put out.

I picked up the chair that was next to me and went to work on ole girl. I stabbed her with a fork. I punched a few teeth down her throat. I went to jail and I was banned from Houston's for life. Shon bonded me right out. Our relationship went downhill after that and I broke up with his ass. He tried me in the worst fuckin' way. I vowed to never let a nigga try me like that again. I moved to Miami and never looked back. Shon never sold the house that he bought us. I sneak to Atlanta frequently and never run into him.

I still have the keys to the house. That's my home when I visit. My name is on the deed. Sphinx is having a birthday party real soon and I'll be visiting. I'm good on Shon Adams. I wish him nothing but the best. It was so hard to move on. I couldn't believe he done that to me. I did move on. It took me some time, but I got over him. I was raised in the church. I stopped going because of the things I was involved in. I prayed so hard that God would remove anything affiliated with Shon out of my life and He did with time.

It was a nightmare. I thought I was going to spend the rest of my life with him. You live, and you learn. I learned so much from that experience. I finally got the courage to move on two years after I moved to Miami. I met Cree, my fiancé, and the love of my life.

He's Haitian too and we share a lot of the same family values. He's a street nigga too. I shook Shon, but I ran into another street nigga. Cree was a different breed and only wanted me. Home was the only place he wanted to be.

My brothers like him, and my mother approve of him. Our wedding is scheduled for March 16, 2019. He's been bugging me for months to set a date. I finally picked one, but I didn't want a fairytale wedding because I didn't have many friends. Cree wanted to give me the wedding of my dreams. I wanted something small and simple.

Shon

Running into Sphinx brought back a lot of memories that I would never forget. My mind instantly traveled to Layla Rene Baptiste. She was the love of my life and I wanted her to be my wife. I wanted that with her. I fucked all that up and I've been paying for it ever since. Vell and Sphinx ran up on me the same day when Layla and I got into it and she was trying to leave me. I wasn't having that shit. I was in love with Layla Baptiste. She had my heart and took it with her when she left.

To be honest I still love her. I never stopped loving her. She took my heart and never gave it back to a nigga. The day she left me I never committed to another female. I've been running through these chicks like it was going out of style. I guess that's how that love shit works. You take one person for granted and they're liable to fuck up your whole life. I know I haven't been the best man to a lot of females out here.

I can't even say it's because of Layla. I had a good woman and let her slip right through my fuckin' hands.

I wanted to right every wrong with Layla if I could. More of the reason why I didn't want my sister getting acquainted with Sphinx. I know Sphinx and I don't want him with my sister at all. I know he'll dog Malone out the same way I did Layla. I put that shit on my OG, that wasn't fuckin' happening. Malone better not know him. I saw how he was looking at her. It was the same way I looked at Layla and I didn't like that shit at all.

It's been years since I've seen Layla. She always crossed my mind, and she was the one that got away. She just upped and left a nigga with no trace. All that shit was my fault though. I got sloppy with my shit. I knew fuckin' with Sidney was going to be a nigga down fall. The moment she showed up at Houston's I knew shit was about to go left. Layla went to jail, I bonded her ass out, and she bailed on a nigga. I would give anything if I could change back the hands of time. I swear to God I would.

It's funny because every now and then life has a way of reminding you of all the fucked-up things you did in the past.

If I wouldn't have seen Sphinx, none of this shit would've crossed my mind. I never got the chance to tell Layla how sorry I was. I always saw Ms. Shaolin in passing but she never had any words for me. I couldn't blame her though, Layla was her only daughter. My selfish ways ran her away.

Chapter 2

Layla

Sphinx is having a party tonight at the Compound. I wasn't going to go because I only go home for the holidays and his birthday. It's so last minute and my fiancé Cree is looking at me like I'm crazy. Leave it to Sphinx to book me a flight that leaves in two hours. I needed a 72-hour notice, but I'll support my brother no matter what.

I was scheduled to touch down in Atlanta a little after 1:00 p.m. Atlanta was always home because I was born and raised there, but I love Miami. It's always nice, no winter, or snow. My brothers said No Cap. Don't bring anything because everything was on them. They didn't have to tell me twice.

It's the middle of the week and I'll probably stay until Friday. I couldn't be away from Cree for too long. He was a little salty about me leaving last minute BUT my brother sent for me, so I was going. He dropped me off at the airport and I kissed him bye. Next stop security.

A two-hour nonstop flight and here I am, Hartsville Jackson Airport. It feels good to be in Atlanta. The vibe was nice, and snow was in the forecast, yuck. Thank God I didn't have to grab any luggage and my rental car was already reserved. I just had to go there to pick it up. I took my phone off airplane mode to call the Trap God himself to let him know that I arrived and to cash app me some money. I needed to get glammed up. He answered on the first ring. He better.

"Hello, you made it?" I missed my brother so much.

"Yep, I'm walking through the airport now, what's the tab because I don't want no bitch weighing up to me tonight." I beamed.

"Whatever you want. I know it's short notice, but I had a concierge grab you a ton of things to pick from. Text me the address to the house so she can get you right."

"Thank you, it's sent."

"I'll see you later." Sphinx is smart. I could relax at the house for a few hours. I need to get my nails done and my hair curled.

Tonight may be a good night. I'm glad I came, if he didn't book the ticket it would've been a no. Let me call OG Vell. He swears that I love Sphinx more. I do because Vell always bossed me around because we were so close in age and he thought that he was my daddy, and he isn't.

Shon

Yona's birthday was today. I didn't have anything special planned for her. We're kicking it and that's about it. I didn't see a future with her. I had no plans to make her my wife. I didn't feel the need to go out my way to make her feel special. Her birthday is just another fuckin' day to me. I gave her two wads full of cash just to shut her ass up. Yona always wanted to be the center of attention. I'm a street nigga and I don't like all eyes on me. If it's to many motherfuckas watching me, that puts a target on my back. A nigga ain't trying to have that.

The worse thing a nigga or bitch can do is become an enemy of mine. I got nothing but time to handle any nigga that wanted to be a casualty of mine. That's the fuckin' end, and the result is a fuckin' casualty. I'm all for Guerrilla Warfare. I'm dying to push a nigga shit back if they wanted to get at me. It's always repercussions for fuckin' with a nigga like me.

I don't move like that anymore, but I will if necessary. Nine times out of ten, I'm either moving a pack or waiting for a few to come in. Securing a bag was my only fuckin' focus.

"Baby, it's a party tonight can we go to celebrate my birthday, please?" She pouted and whined. I hate to bust Yona's bubble, but the only celebrating she was getting was the wads of cash I gave her, and this dick if she wanted it tonight.

"Come on Yona, you know I don't do clubs. Take your girls with you and I'll get y'all a section," I argued. Yona wanted to hit me with the sad face. I'm not trying to be in the club with Yona posted up on some relationship type shit. I ain't trying to give out the wrong impression. There are boundaries and she was over stepping those motherfuckas.

"I want you to come with me Shon. We can fuck like we're together, but we can't be seen together?" She argued. Yona placed her hands on her hips and rolling her eyes like I really gave a fuck. I swear I'm not trying to go there with her but she's asking for it.

"Yona don't do that shit shawty. You know what the fuck it is with us. I ain't got to fuck you shawty at all. A nigga ain't never been pressed for pussy. Pussy is given to me on a platter. I curve bitches all day because pussy isn't the only thing on a nigga mind.

We're fuckin' because you wanted to fuck me, and you wanted to fuck with a nigga like me. You approached me, and the pussy was the only thing you had to offer a nigga.

You got to come better than that shawty. I told you it ain't no relationship out the gate. I'm not trying to settle down at all. If you want something, don't I fuckin' give it to you? You ain't fuckin' a nigga for free shawty, your hands are always out. I'm a nigga that make shit happen shawty. If you want to go to the party, you can, and I'll pay for that shit."

"Shon you work all the time, loosen up, please. I don't ask for much. Can I get a little time outside of the bedroom? I got something real special planned for you afterwards. I want to be your personal porn star." Yona unbuckled my pants and started topping me off.

She gave me some head that was so fuckin' sloppy and wet. I didn't even know her mouth got that wet. Hell, yeah, I'll make an appearance at the club.

Layla

Sphinx party was nice. I can't believe Shon, Dino and Twin were there. It's been years since I've seen them. If you saw one of them, trust me the other two were near. Then we locked eyes with each other. It was crazy. He read my mind and I read his. He was with someone. I was more than a little bothered. I can admit that. Why was I bothered, and I'm engaged? I shouldn't even be feeling like this. I wanted to ask Malone who she was. I wanted to fuckin' know. Whoever she was, she couldn't have been too much because his eyes stayed on me. He nodded his head at me, and I nodded mine back.

His VIP was too close to Sphinx's. I hadn't seen him in years and to see him tonight, my heart dropped. Why does he still have this effect on me? Oh my gosh, every feeling that I had hidden, were reappearing. I stayed on the dance floor the whole night because I couldn't be that close to Shon. My feet were killing me. I couldn't wait to run to the car to kick these shoes off. My flight was scheduled to leave Tuesday, but I'm leaving tomorrow. I just knew something bad was about to happen.

I could feel it. Malone wasn't making it any better by telling me to go over there. I wish the fuck I would go over there because IF a bitch says something smart, I'm coming up out of these heels and beating ass.

As soon as the party was over, I gave my brothers a hug. I was on the track team tonight. I ran to valet, damn near busting my ass to get my car and pull the fuck off. My mind was in a million places. I couldn't be anywhere near Shon. It's crazy because I was just reminiscing about this man a few weeks ago. I haven't seen him in about six years. Anytime Sphinx and Vell decided to throw a big party they're cleaning money and I'm always in attendance. Shon has never been to a party. It's crazy. Why was he at this party?

I thought tonight would be like any other night when I partied with my brothers, but it wasn't. It was so much tension between Shon and me, that only we could feel it. If a knife was an option, it still couldn't cut the tension between us. A lot of shit needed to be said. It wouldn't get said because well, I had too much pride to even speak with him. I still loved him despite the things he did to me. I could never treat people how they treat me. My heart has a mind of her own. If I wouldn't have seen him, I wouldn't even be feeling like this. I'll still fuck him. I need to shake these feelings quick.

Shon had to know voodoo. I believe he put something on me when he looked at me tonight. He had that voodoo dick. I shouldn't even be thinking about his dick at all. He invaded my mind for tonight. It's cool because tomorrow memories of him would be foreign. I promised Sphinx and Vell that I would cook for the, but. I'll have to take a rain check on that. I'm a bitch on the run. We'll have to catch up another time. I'm sure it wouldn't be long before Shon tries to contact me. As soon as I get home, I'm deactivating all social media. I didn't want him to find me at all. I had a feeling not to come here. I should've trusted my feelings. I guess this was why.

Chapter 3

Shon

I'm glad I showed my face at Sphinx's party. Normally I wouldn't have come out tonight, but it was Yona's birthday and she damn near begged me too. I ran into the love of my life all because of her. Sphinx was throwing the biggest party in the city. Of course, I had to come through, since it was my situation's birthday. Sphinx's VIP section was right beside mine. I saw a face that looked familiar. I can spot Layla from anywhere and her measurements hadn't changed. Dino and Twin thought I was tripping, but I kept saying to myself, that's her. I could feel it. Me and my niggas were sitting back blowing. I started breaking down my weed and I looked up, as I licked my blunt. I looked again, and she looked at me. I nodded my head acknowledging her. Damn, that was Layla.

Of course, I wanted to say something to her. I couldn't stop looking at her. My eyes followed her everywhere she went. If she was with a nigga, I was bodying his ass on sight. She knew I was coming for her ass. That's why she hauled ass. I let her get away from me one time, it won't be a second. I put that shit on everything I love.

"Where are we headed?" She asked. Ugh, I forgot she was even in the car with me. My mind was on Layla Baptiste. I was finding her ass tonight.

"Your house?"

"Why?" She pouted and whined. I don't have to answer to any fuckin' body but my OG. I turned the music up. Yona and I don't have a title, but I couldn't tell her that I was trying to get up with Layla. She'll act a damn fool. I had to see what was up with her. I haven't seen her in years. Even if it was just a what's up. I wanted that. My phone rang, and it was my nigga, Dino.

"Yo, tell me you have some good news?" I could hear it in his voice, he got the drop.

"Shon, I followed her like you told me too. You wouldn't believe where she's staying at?" He chuckled. I didn't like that.

"Dino, send me that shit now," I argued. He knew I was fuming hot.

"Bet," I looked at my phone. Yona's nosey ass was looking too. Damn shawty checks your phone and not mine, you'll fuck around and get your feelings hurt. Layla was slick as fuck.

"What was that about?" She asked and turned around in her seat facing me.

"My business, and not fuckin' yours. Mind the business that pays you. I'm meeting Dino and Twin I'm about to handle some business. I'll see you tomorrow."

"On my fucking birthday Shon, you have to handle some business?" She argued.

"On your fuckin' birthday Yona. Money talks and bullshit walks a thousand miles. Yes, because my bills don't pay themselves. You for damn sure don't pay any. Yeah, I got to Jugg." I argued. The fuck she thought this was.

"Fuck you, Shon." She spat. She wanted me to fuck her, but I wanted to fuck something else.

"I'll be back tomorrow to do just that, I want that pussy hot and ready," I dropped Yona off. She slammed my door hard as fuck. I pulled off doing a doughnut. What the fuck was Layla doing at our old house and how did she get in? I never changed the locks, but I could've sworn when she left, she dropped those keys. I guess not if she still had access. I would've never thought to look there. Daddy was on his way home.

I missed the fuck out of Layla real shit. I'll never admit it, but I do. I acted for years as if I was good, but I wasn't. I care about her. I always hoped that she was doing good. Our break up fucked her up. A boy will never admit when he's wrong, but a grown ass man will. I'm man enough to admit that shit now. I see the error of my ways. Vell, Sphinx, and I were beefing for a minute behind Layla. I was young and dumb as fuck back then. I couldn't give her what she wanted. These hoes didn't give a fuck about me. They wanted my bag and some dick if I was offering it.

I finally made it to our house. I haven't been to this house in about five years. All my mail goes to a P.O BOX and the mortgage is paid for. I cashed out on this house years ago. When Layla and I moved in, the neighbors couldn't stand it because we were some young rich niggas. The utilities are on auto draft. I pay a landscaper to keep the yard cut. I can't even tell you the last time I've been here.

I sat in the driveway for about thirty minutes debating rather or not I wanted to pull in the garage. Fuck it, if she came here then she didn't plan on leaving. I hit the garage and her car was parked inside.

I made my way upstairs to our old bedroom and she was in the bed looking at TV eating grapes and sipping a water. I stood in the door looking at her. She finally looked toward the door. She didn't say anything. She continued watching TV.

"Layla, what the fuck are you doing in my house?"

"Shon, why are you following me? My name is on the deed too. I'm in my house." She argued. Still feisty and mean as hell.

"How you been?" I asked. I wanted to know everything.

"Fine," she sassed. She was giving me a one liner. I came inside the room and started undressing. I could feel her looking at me. She knew what it was. I've been waiting on this day for years. This is my house too and I'm not going anywhere. Layla got from underneath the covers, she was naked as the day she was born. I'm not even surprised. She grabbed her grapes and water. She started to exit the room. I jumped in front of her, and she tried to go around me. I stood in the door way blocking her.

"Move Shon." She argued. Why was she mad at me? I haven't done shit to her.

"What I do, damn can I join you?"

"I don't think that's a great idea, let me leave and I'll find somewhere else to stay." She kept trying to move around me. I wasn't having that. Her chest was heaving up and down. Layla knows how this shit goes. We've been here before. Leaving me again wasn't an option.

"You don't have to leave, where do you think you're going this time of night?"

"Shon, all I want to do is relax. Anytime I come to the city, I stay at my house. It's been that way for years. We see each other for the first time in a long time, and you pop up here? Why are you here and don't say it's because of me? You and I both know you don't come here. Could you please leave my home?"

"I'm not stopping you from relaxing. I still care about you, Layla. I still love you. I wanted to catch up with you to see how you've been. You've been hiding from a nigga for years. This is my house too and I'm not leaving." I argued.

"Why would I need to hide from you? I always lay my head here. I've been coming here for the past seven years. I haven't run into you one time. It's not coincidental. I'll leave since you want to be here for tonight."

"Yeah, I had Dino to follow you. Layla damn you don't have to leave. It's too late for you to be out."

"I can take care of myself. I don't need anybody following me."

"Look Layla, you're not going anywhere this time of night. I won't bother you or do anything you don't want me to do."

"Shon, how about you leave? I'm going back home tomorrow anyway."

"Where's home, Layla?" I asked. I wanted to know where she was living.

"Why and can you just move out my way? I'll go to my mother's house," she argued. She turned around and grabbed her clothes and started putting them on."

"I'm not trying to fight with you Layla, I swear I'm not. I'm sorry. I know I'm probably the last nigga you want to see. I had to come and see you. I missed the shit out of you. It's been years."

"I'm not fighting with you Shon. Why would you come here? You know what the fuck you did to me? I don't want to see you. I didn't miss you. I got to go, and it was good seeing you," she argued. She tried to walk past me. I wasn't letting her leave out of here like this.

"Layla, I said I was sorry. You're not leaving out of this house. It's almost 5:00 a.m., and these streets ain't safe. I'll sleep on the couch or in the guest room, and you can have our room. I'll give you that."

"Okay." She sassed. She slammed the door in my face. Layla got me fucked up. As soon as I think she's asleep I'm going in that room. She knows she missed a nigga. She couldn't even look me in the eye. I know the way we ended things was kind of fucked up, but I still love her. That's why I told her that. She still had my heart and I had hers.

Layla

Ugh why did he have to come over here? What happened to ole girl? I swore it felt like he just took my heart from me all over again. I couldn't be near Shon at all. I had to get back to Miami ASAP. I couldn't really look at him like I wanted to in the club but damn he's gotten better with time. A full beard, muscle, and all chocolate. I'll leave tomorrow or maybe sneak out tonight. He was too sneaky for me. I wouldn't even be able to sleep with him being so close to me. I cut the TV off and prayed that sleep would consume me.

I was sleeping well until I felt somebody get in the bed with me. I tried to ignore it and play like I was still sleeping until he wrapped his arms around me. I moved instantly, and he grabbed me.

"I'm sorry I miss the shit out of you Layla. One night, that's all I ask." He whispered in my ear. He sent chills through my body. I ignored him and scooted away from him. It could never be an us again. I'm taken. Ain't shit single about me. Even if I was, I wouldn't give him the time of day. I'll never forget what he did to me.

I ignored him. Why was he doing this. It only complicates things. It felt good to be wrapped in Shon's arms, but I will never forget how he did me. I forgave him years ago. I had too because I wanted to give Cree all of me. This is the reason that I wanted to go to my mother's house. I knew where things would lead to and he's already in my bed and between my legs. I wasn't turning down any head from him. This pussy he wasn't about to slide in it. I can't cheat on Cree. Let me stop him. Cree is a good nigga and I would never cheat on him. I would leave before I had the chance to. He doesn't deserve this.

"Shon stop we can't do this." I moaned. He was sucking the soul out of me. My legs were shaking.

"Stop for what?" He asked.

"I'm not a cheater and I can't cheat on him with you?"

"Layla, I don't give a fuck about him. Does he know that when you come home, that you stay in a house that we shared?"

"I care, Shon don't fight me on this please," I moaned. I tried to get up, but he wouldn't let me. He had a tight grip on my thighs while he continued to eat my pussy as his life depended on it. I swear my soul left my body.

"Don't make me cheat please. I don't want to do this."

"Layla, I don't give a fuck about that nigga. I don't owe him shit and he doesn't owe me shit. Look me in my face and tell me you want me to stop. Layla, if you don't want this then I might ease up."

"Shon, I don't want this." He laughed at me and continued to eat my pussy. He's just forcing me to cheat and I don't want to do this. He raised up and started looking at me. I closed my eyes because I didn't want to look at him. He knows voodoo. I'm convinced.

"You mad," he laughed. I attempted to get up and he pressed me back down on the bed and started kissing me. Oh my God, I felt like I was dying. His kisses were so sensual and sexual. I wasn't kissing him back.

"You know you mine right. I'm not letting you go. Call that pussy ass nigga and tell him it's over. Wherever home is, you ain't going back." He argued. He just knew we were going to be together after this. Shon ended up sliding his dick inside of me, and it was big like I remembered it. A few soft moans escaped my lips. My pussy had a mind of her own too. She was extra wet for Shon.

"We need a condom?" I moaned.

"For what? I've never strapped up with you before and I'm not about to now." He argued.

"Shon, we haven't been together in years. I'm sure you have a shit load of kids and you've been hitting females raw, so we need a condom." I argued.

"If you wanted to know if I have any kids then answer is no. I'm ready to make some now with you. Let's go half on a baby Layla. I have a few fuck buddies, but I never give them 100% pure beef. I always strap up. I want to give you this beef."

"You have a few too many fuck buddies for me," I flipped Shon over on his back side. He wrapped his lips around my breast, and his arms around my waist. I jumped up and ran to the shower and locked the door because he was right on my heels. I couldn't get caught up with Shon again. I've come to far. He was my weakness and I refuse to be weak over him again.

He started banging on the bathroom door. He should be glad he had the chance to even feel me again.

I took a hot shower because I needed to wash Shon off me. Tonight, I would be changing the forecast. I would be in Miami with Cree, the love of my life. I feel bad that I did this much with Shon.

Shon

Layla knew she was teasing a nigga. I wanted her bad as fuck. She kept throwing it up in my face that she didn't want to cheat. Fuck her nigga. He doesn't owe me shit and I don't owe him. If Layla was his woman, I was taking the pussy tonight. She was mine first and she'll forever be mine. She locked the bathroom door like I couldn't get in. I always get what I want. Layla knew that when she saw me, she knew I was coming for her. That's why she ran out. We were together for ten years, what did she expect? I know our past is fucked up and I fucked her over. I shouldn't have, but I'm older now and a lot wiser.

I'm thirty-one years old. I fuck different broads from time to time, but I'm not committing to anyone. I'll commit to Layla. I grabbed the same butter knife that I used to get in my bedroom and popped the lock on the bathroom. I yanked the curtain back and hopped right in with her. She was surprised to see me, nothing can stop me from getting at her.

"Stop playing with me," I smacked Layla on her ass and she turned her head and looked at me. I pushed up on her from behind. I grabbed the towel and soap to wash up. The water felt good up against my body, but Layla was about to feel better. She tried to rush out. I grabbed her by the waist. Soon she'll find out that she wasn't going anywhere.

"It's been my pussy for years. Today ain't no different." I backed Layla into the base of the shower. She knew it was about to go down and nobody was about to stop me.

"Shon I'm not your fuck buddy. I'm in a committed relationship." She argued. I don't give a fuck.

"You don't have to be my fuck buddy, you can be whatever you want to be. If you're ready to be my wife, I'll give you that title. If you want to be my lady, you can be that too. Whatever you want just tell me." I meant that shit and she knew. I've been playing games with these females for years because I wanted Layla. I'm done with all the games and bull shit.

"Shon, you, -" I cut Layla off. I put my hand over her mouth, because she was doing too much talking. My other hand roamed the pussy that laid between her legs. I finger fucked Layla wet. I watched her bite the inside of her jaw. She had too much pride to bite her lip. She started moaning and I knew I had her right where I wanted her. She bit my hand.

"Put it in." She begged and moaned.

"I thought you didn't want to cheat," I asked? Layla grabbed my dick and put it in her warm wet pussy just like I knew she would.

I picked her up and carried her to the room. I tossed her on the bed and I dived in that pussy immediately. I'm about to put in overtime with this pussy. I stroked her long, deep, and hard. I liked the way her juices coated my dick. I guess she got tired of me teasing her because she started grinding on me and throwing that pussy back at a nigga. Ten years later and she still fits me like a glove. This was my pussy and Layla knew that.

"Did I tell you to throw it back? You're still hard headed. I'm in control remember that." I chuckled. Layla rolled her eyes at me. Each time she would attempt to throw it back and grind on my dick, I would dig deeper and deeper. She would then slow down and ease the fuck up. She knew I was a beast in the bedroom, ain't shit changed. I knew when she couldn't handle it, because she would squirm, and a few tears escaped the corner of her eyes. It's been years since we've been together, so I was taking my time with this pussy. Layla knew it wasn't no turning back after this. If it was another nigga involved, he wouldn't be in the picture for too long. I wasn't having that.

Layla

What did I just do? I can't blame it on the alcohol. I'm way smarter than what I just did. I wanted to fuck Shon. He asked for it. I fucked him into a coma. I just cheated on my nigga for a nigga that's not about shit. I knew better but he was so fuckin' persistent. I rolled over and looked at Shon. Damn, he was so sexy. Why did he have to be so fuckin' fine?

"Layla why are you staring at me?" he yawned. Shon wrapped his arms around my waist making sure that I didn't bust a move on him. He knew me. He knew when he went to sleep, I was dipping on his ass. This was never supposed to happen. He wouldn't let up.

"Is it a crime?" I sassed. He knew why I was looking at him. I can't believe I fucked him.

"I don't want you to leave. I miss you. I love you Layla." I ignored him and placed a few soft kisses on his lips. I couldn't help myself. His lips were perfect, and they feel even better. He grabbed the back of head and forced his tongue down my throat. Damn, why did he fuck up? He was never this affectionate and romantic. I guess it's true, some niggas do get better with time.

It's too bad this little thing must end. He's a fine specimen to look at. Shon was the perfect shade of caramel. His body is covered with muscles. The sight of the sweat running down his chest from our workout did something to me. He was trying to learn my body again. I don't know why because this was my first and last one-night stand. The death strokes were hypnotizing me. We went at it for hours. I sweated my hair out. Thank God my bald-headed ass had good hair. It just curled up.

Shon always had that voodoo dick. I tiptoed out of bed, quietly grabbed my bag and shoes and ran down the steps. I couldn't be here when Shon woke up. I needed to take a shower to handle my hygiene. I had to wash Shon off me, but that would have to wait. I jumped in the car, hit the garage button, and pulled out as fast as I could. I would never come back here again. He had Dino follow me, why? I didn't even get the chance to speak with Tory, she was cool. Shon, Dino, and Twin have been best friends for as long as I can remember. I'm not surprised they'll do anything for each other.

My mother's house was out of the question. I couldn't go there because that's the first place Shon would look. I could lay low at my brother's house. He would never ask them about me because of our history. I didn't feel like arguing with Vell. He treats me like a child and I'm not his fuckin' child. He's only three years older than me. Of course, I was calling Sphinx. My phone was connected to the Bluetooth when he picked up on the first ring.

"Good afternoon." His voice blared through the speakers. I could tell he was up moving around.

"Where are you?" I beamed.

"Moving around Trapping, what's up?" He asked.

"Text me the code to the house in North Druid Hills."

"Why?" He chuckled. What was so funny? I just asked for the code.

"Does it matter Sphinx, I need to take a shower and change clothes?" I sighed. I swear he was doing too much right now.

"Why couldn't you do it at the house you've been doing it?" He asked. I looked at the phone. I can't believe him right now.

"Fuck it, I'll get a room since you're being a detective. I bet you don't give Vell the 21 questions you just asked me?" I argued. I don't have time for this shit.

"Layla, if you can't keep it real with yourself, you can't keep real with nobody else. You're hiding something." He argued and chuckled. He hides shit all the time. Somebody must have pissed in his cheerios this morning.

"You know what Sphinx, fuck this. I'm the oldest give me the code DAMN. I fucked the shit out of Shon last night. Is that what you wanted to hear?" I argued.

"Yep, I knew it. Cree's a good nigga Layla, you shouldn't have cheated on him. The dog shit run through our blood." He laughed.

"I'm nothing like you and Vell. I haven't fucked a lot of men. I've fucked Shon before so that doesn't count. I just circled back last night because that nigga was persistent. I gave him everything he asked for and dipped."

"Whatever makes you feel better. I sent the code to your phone. I'll swing by in a few."

"Okay." I sighed. I love Sphinx and I hate his petty ass at the same time. He knew what the fuck he was doing. He wanted to give me the fifth degree just to take a shower. Lord forgive me. What a night. Shon did a number on me last night. We both wanted it.

NINE MONTHS LATER

Chapter 4

Layla

I could've sworn I was asleep and taking a much-needed nap in peace until Shon rudely interrupted me. It's already hard for me to sleep. I can't sleep at night because that's when the baby is the most active. It's like she knows when her father is at home. Shon will talk to my stomach and she acts up. I'll be so glad when I have her. I can't wait to meet my princess. I can already tell she's going to be a daddy's girl.

"Shon can you please stop, I'm tired," I moaned. I rotated my hips in his mouth. He wanted to wake me up by eating my pussy. I was for damn sure going to feed him. I was on the verge of cumin'. Shon bit my pussy lips with his two front teeth and gave it a little tug. I came instantly on his face. My body shook. I needed that.

"I thought you wanted me to stop Layla?" He asked and laughed. I swore I hated him sometimes, but I loved him to death. He knew what he was doing.

"I did Shon. I'm trying to get some rest before our daughter gets here." I pouted. Shon knew how hard it was for me to go to sleep. He didn't have any problems going to sleep because he wasn't the one that was carrying a child, I was.

"Layla, I'm trying to get as much pussy ass I can before our daughter gets here." I'm trying to get as much dick as possible too.

"Like wise, you better get all you can because when she gets here. It'll be no pussy for fourteen weeks. I'm not trying to have another baby." I mumbled. Shon rose up and looked at me. I know he heard me.

If Shon thinks that I'm going to be having all these babies without a real commitment, he has another thing coming. I meant that shit.

He rose up from between my legs and wiped his mouth. I watched him out the corner of my eye.

"What are you saying Layla?" Shon was looking at me and stroking his beard. He knew what the fuck I was saying. He's far from dumb.

"I don't want to get pregnant right after I have Shalani." I sassed. I raised up from the bed and went to the bathroom. I needed a shower. Shon was right on my heels. I'm not trying to argue with him, it's too early. He knows what he needs to do.

"What's wrong with that Layla? You know I'm going to take care of you and my kids for the rest of my life." He argued. I've been with Shon for a long ass time, most of my life since I was 15 or 16 years old. I'm not about to play these games with him this time around. He placed the ring on my finger, but I need the real thing. Don't put this shit on my finger just to scare off the next man.

"Nothing's wrong with-it Shon but I'm not going to be your girlfriend nor baby momma forever," I argued. Shon walked up on me and backed me in the corner. He cupped my face making me look at him. I tried to break the gaze. He cupped my face with a tight grip.

"Layla, you don't have to talk in circles. You always have my attention. I didn't do any of that shit I did for you to be my baby momma. I always wanted you to be my wife. If you're ready to get married, we can do that. He explained. He heard what the fuck I said, and I meant that shit too.

"Okay, Shon." I pouted. I've been with Shon way too fucking long to still be his girlfriend. I don't give a fuck how many years we were apart. We picked back up where we left off.

"I'm serious Layla." He sighed. We exchanged a very passionate kiss. Shon and I took a hot steamy shower. He had to handle some business on the Eastside. I he had to drop some work off to OG Lou. I knew he would be gone for a few hours. I didn't have anything to do.

I grabbed my phone and seen I had a few missed calls from Malone and Leilani. I had plans to get up with Leah and Malone for lunch and just kick it. I called Malone back first to see what she wanted. I knew she was up to no good.

"What's up Lonnie? I've been calling you all morning. I guess Mr. Baptiste got you tied up." I beamed. I could tell she was smiling by her tone. I swore I thought I'd never see the day when someone locked Sphinx down. Who knew it would be Malone?

"Layla, stop! Mr. Baptiste has been gone all morning. Thank God. My baby Samaya is sick so she's been laying up under me all morning and I'm on mommy duty. Laylin and Lateef are asleep. Jah and Kennedy are at school. I heard about you early this morning," she laughed.

"I haven't done anything." I laughed. Shon couldn't wait to run and tell Malone about our conversation not knowing she was going to come back and tell me. It's always us versus them. I'm not surprised he left mad, but he'll be all right.

"Layla, he said that you tried him," she laughed. Malone thought this was the funniest shit.

"Malone, am I wrong? Shon and I have been together forever. The only person I ever been with besides him was Cree. At this point, we should know rather a marriage was in the cards for us or not? If it's not let me get the fuck on. I hope we didn't circle back for me just to have his child and do the things that we did 10 years ago." I argued. Malone let Sphinx know what it was off the rip. She didn't want to be another one of his baby mommas. I don't blame her.

"No, you're not wrong at all Layla, I'm riding with you right or wrong. I don't see what the fuck he's waiting on, especially after he slid that ring back on your finger."

"Malone, that's my fuckin' point. What are we waiting on? I can't make a nigga do shit he doesn't want to do. Nor am I begging him to marry me. Part of the reason why I left years ago was that I didn't see a future with him. I could've stayed here to see if things would get better, but I didn't. I went to go find myself and to be honest, that was the best thing I could've done because I was settling with Shon back then. I know my worth and I don't have to settle for shit. If Shon can't give me what I want, there are plenty of men that's out here that can.

He has until after Shalani is born to make something happen or I'm going back to Miami. I swear Malone, I'm gone. I won't keep her away from him, but this shit with Shon and I got going on will be over. I got my shit together, so why would I continue to wait for Shon to get his together? I'm not doing that shit anymore." I swear it felt good to get that shit off my chest.

"Layla don't do that, please don't. Shon loves you and that nigga was lost without you for years. He was running around out here blind. You're the only woman that he's ever committed too. I'm not taking up for him because he's my brother. I'm a woman before anything. He loves you. Don't for one second ever doubt that. Marriage is in the cards for the two of you. He did entirely too much to get you, to lose you. I know it wasn't in vain. Hopefully, it's soon before I magically get pregnant again." She explained. Malone wasn't fooling me. I knew she was pregnant again. She was throwing a hint. I really appreciate her for listening and always being there for me when I needed her the most. I couldn't ask for a better sister.

"Malone, does Sphinx know that you're pregnant again? Shon better make some shit happen. I swear I'm not playing with him. I'm ready to get married. Do you know how long I've waited to marry the love of my life? Even when we were apart, I didn't think we would ever find our way back to each other. It happened."

"True love always reigns supreme Layla." Malone and I finished talking and laughing for a few more minutes. Our lunch date was canceled since Samaya is sick. I was on one today, maybe it's the pregnancy and the hormones.

I was way past tired of being pregnant and Shon's girlfriend or trophy wife. I needed the real thing. If he had no plans to do that. He can get the fuck on. It's a new day and Layla Rene Baptiste has woken up. My phone alerted me that I had a text. It was from Shon. Let's see what he has to say.

My Heart - I love you Layla and you know that. I want you to be my wife. I got you, trust me. I'm going to make it happen. Be patient with me. I don't want to keep living this life without you having my last name. You're the woman that has the key to my heart.

Shon

Layla is tripping hard. It must be the pregnancy. My daughter is wearing her out and she's snapping on me. I almost forgot who she was for a minute. Of course, I was going to marry her, why would she think that I wasn't? The only reason I haven't done it yet is that I don't want her saying it's too soon. If she's ready than I'm ready. Layla's words have been tugging at my heart since I left the house earlier. The thought of losing Layla fucks with my mental and I don't like the pain that I'm feeling in my chest. I've placed my life on the line for her plenty of times. Marriage changes the game for me.

The day I say I do I'm done with anything affiliated with the streets. I've been hustling since I was fifteen. I'm damn near thirty-three. I don't have to do this shit anymore. I'm blessed to be a part of the Baptiste Cartel when I say I do. I'm not fucking with that anymore. I'm going to be a real family man. I have a few legit businesses' and plan on opening a few more. I had to stop by my mother' s house. I needed her to cook up this dope for me. I can't keep paying

OG Lou $1,000.00 per brick she cooks up and breaks down. She's robbing the fuck out of me.

"Shon, what the fuck is wrong with you? Why are you in a daze? You need to focus, it's a lot of shit going on out here in these streets. Get your head in the fuckin' game. Look, you need to find somebody else to cook up your dope because I'm leaving for Haiti in three hours. Lorenzo wants me to go out there for a few weeks, so we can spend some time together," she argued and sassed. My OG thought she was grown since she had a boyfriend and shit. I wasn't filling it because nobody can replace my father. I'm not having that shit. Why the fuck she needs to be gone for three weeks? Why couldn't he come to the US? It's hurricane season. She needs to keep her ass at home, but I'll have to learn to accept that he's gone and never coming back. My mother deserves to be happy and I'll never deny her that.

"Ma, Layla is tripping on a nigga hard talking about she's not going to be my girlfriend forever. OG Lou charges too much. $1000.00 for a brick gawd damn she's robbing the fuck out of me like I'm not her grandson. You may need to postpone your trip. It's hurricane season and I can't let you get caught up."

"Shon you know I'm not afraid to die because I can't wait until the day that I can see my husband again. I'm running through those pearly gates to see Big Shon. It better not be a bitch in his face. I'm grown, I do what I want Shon. I don't blame Layla for tightening up on your ass. Why are you waiting to marry her? See that's your problem. Young niggas got the game wrong. A real woman doesn't have to wait around for you to finally decide to marry her. She'll leave you. Shon, don't let her leave you again. I hope you didn't think she was going to continue to wait?"

Chapter 5

Leah

Lately I've been doing my own thing and staying out the way. Vell and I have been broken up for a few months now. I can't even get over him properly because he's everywhere. I told Malone and Layla they wouldn't see me for a while because I'm trying to get over him. I can't do that if he's always around and I'm always seeing him. It's necessary that I fall back from my girls for a little while. These past few months I've had nothing but time on my hands. I wanted to do something with myself, but I didn't know what.

I've always been good with fashion and make up. As soon as Vell and I broke up, everything he brought me I posted for sale pictures on my Instagram and Facebook. I made a shit load of cash off the items they purchased. Vell was all in my DM's telling me to stop selling the shit that he bought me because it was brought with love.

I blocked his ass. Fashion and make-up have always been my thing. I'm thinking about opening an online store and maybe a boutique later. Every outfit or piece of clothing that I uploaded to my social media account somebody wanted to purchase it.

I'm headed to the post office now to send off a few orders. I had a trunk full of stuff that needed to be shipped to my customers. It's crazy because the only thing I ever sold was Kush and pills. It feels good to be making some money off something legit. I swear the few customers that I have is what keeps me going. They're my motivation in this crazy world that I'm existing and trying to live in. The thought came to me all sudden. It's that the thrill of moving packs doesn't excite me anymore.

I've made so much money these past few years. I don't want to do it anymore because I've seen a lot of my associates go down with this shit. Why not get paid to do something that you love? My grandmother would kill me if she knew what the fuck I was doing. I finally made it to the post office to send off these orders. I would have to make two trips inside. I felt a tap on my shoulder. I turned around and looked to see who it was.

I had a mean scowl on my face. I don't feel like being bothered. I just want to ship my packages off and go to Starbucks to grab a fresh cup of coffee. Shit, this nigga could be trying to rob me for all I know.

"Hey, Ms. Lady, can I take some of that off your hands," he asked. Damn, he was fine as hell. I could tell he was from New Orleans the way he said, lady. He dragged it out a lil bit.

"No thank you I'm good." I beamed and put a small smile on my face. He needed to get the fuck away from me ASAP. He was looking at me and stroking his beard.

"I hear you Ms. Lady, but I can't allow you to carry these things all by yourself. I'll be less than a man to do that. My mother and father raised me right, and to always be a gentleman. I'm helping you rather you want me to or not." He explained. He started taking my stuff out of my trunk. I had to move out his way because he was determined and persistent.

"My name is Malik, by the way, it's nice to meet you, Ms. Lady.

"It's nice to meet you to Malik. I go by the name of Leah. Thank you." I extended my hand out for him to shake it. He gave me a firm hand shake. He was staring me in my eyes. I tried so hard to break the gaze. Malik carried my stuff into the post office and sat my boxes on the counter. He was standing right behind me, making me uncomfortable. My palms were sweaty. I had to wipe them on my jeans.

Another cashier opened a line and she went ahead and took Malik. Thank God. He threw me off my square and I didn't like that shit at all. In all my years of living, I've never met a man that had this type of effect on me. I finally approached the counter and shipped all my packages off. When the cashier gave me my receipts, I walked to my car to scan them on my phone through USPS, so my customers could track the shipping on their purchases. I heard a tap at my window and I grabbed my gun from my armrest. I looked up and it was Malik with a small smile beamed on my face. I rolled the window down to see what he wanted. He can't be running up on me like this. "Hey, what's up?"

"You Ms. Lady. I'm trying to get to know you. Can I take you out on a date one day," he asked?

"What's makes you think I'm single? I could have a man." I chuckled. Little does he know I have a crazy ass EX. Malik ran his hands through his beard. He was turning me on in the worse way. I could tell he was a few years older than me. He was about to say something smart.

"Leah do you have a man? If so, your man should've never let you out of his presence if I'm combing these streets. Where's your ring, Leah? Call your man up and let me ask him if I can take you out?" He asked. Oh, this motherfucka is crazy for real. He's very persistent, but I think I like him.

"Malik one date that's it. I just got out of something. So, I'm a little skeptical about going out on dates. I'm cooling it for right now and I'm doing my own little thing."

"I feel you Ms. Lady. Let me take you out on one date to get your mind off the bull shit."

"I hear you, Malik."

"I want you to listen to Leah." Malik and I exchanged numbers. He pulled off in a white two door

Bentley coupe. Malik was fine as hell too. His skin was the color of Georgia maple syrup. Tattoos covered his forearms. I could tell he smoked good. Kush was the cologne he wore. His eyes were red and glossy, but they were the color of Hennessy Brown. His hair was cut low. Yeah, he was something to look at. His voice and appearance had me mesmerized.

I finally made it home two hours later. I had a few missed calls from Malone and Layla. I would call them back later. I had a text from a 504 number. It had to be Malik. I changed into some comfortable clothes and made me a cup of warm tea. I took a seat on my sofa, grabbed my phone and replied to the text he sent. He had an iPhone too and he was responding. I locked his name in my phone under Hot boy because he was from Louisiana.

Hot boy - Can I take you out on a date tonight Ms. Lady?

I had to think hard about that. Lawd I guess I could go. Malik was doing something to me.

He must know voodoo because I could hear him call me Ms. Lady through the phone. I'm single, why not. I don't have anything else to do. I sent him a text back.

Me - Maybe?

I guess he didn't like my response because my phone instantly started ringing. I didn't answer on the first ring. He probably was mad because he was expecting me to say yes. I decided to let him sweat a little, so I answered on the third ring. He's probably used to women throwing themselves at him. Not me.

"Hello." I sighed. I had a small smile on my face.

"Maybe Leah, what the fuck is that supposed to mean?" He asked. Shit, what the fuck does it sound like?

"I don't know Malik, we don't know each other. I could be a serial killer and you want to take me out? Shit, you could be a serial killer," I chuckled. I meant that shit too. Niggas ain't just taking females out on dates and shit.

"Leah, chill out. I'm a killer, but I'm not trying to kill you. Let a nigga in, so I can put some of this good loving on you baby.

You're too fine to be a killer, Ms. Lady. Can I take you out to dinner baby," he asked? Damn, he was a smooth talker and he had a way with words.

"Okay, Malik. I hope I don't regret this. I'm not ready to date yet. I am open to conversation."

"Thank you, baby. You know I'm that nigga lil Juvie. We can converse and then we can date. Shoot me your address so I can scoop you." What have I gotten myself into? Why did he want to pick me up? I could've met him somewhere. The last thing I need is for Vell to magically appear over here and I'm smiling all in Malik's face, because of the way he's calling me baby. He makes a bitch just want to throw him the panties and slide all down the dick.

I still have flash backs about what happened to Cohen. I cared about him too. I didn't want that for Malik. I don't even know what to wear. I thumbed through my closet and grabbed a pair of distressed True Religion Jeans, the matching button-down shirt, and a pair of Giuseppe pumps out of the closet. I had to do my hair and all this extra shit. Thank God I just got a fresh sew in yesterday.

Malik is a different breed. The only time I get draped up is to go to the club. I don't think I've ever been on a date before with a hood nigga. I couldn't stop laughing. That was the funniest shit to me. I couldn't even cake my face with make-up. I didn't want to overdo it. I went natural and nude. Malik sent me a text asking me for my unit number. I grabbed my mink coat, he wasn't getting my unit number. As soon as I opened the door. I ran smack dead into Malik. He pulled me into his arms.

"I asked for your address. Baby, you ignored that shit. I had to show you how real shit gets." Damn Malik is aggressive as fuck. I like that shit. It's a turn, I can't even lie. He smelled so good. I could tell he was built nice but being held in his arms felt so good. I had to step back for a minute and take him in. I was caught up because I couldn't understand, how did he know where I lived? The flowers were beautiful.

"Malik, how do you know where I live?" I asked. I needed to know because he caught me off guard and I didn't like that shit at all.

"I know a lot of shit. I was trying to surprise you, but let me guess? You're not used to surprises. I won't over step my boundaries anymore."

"I love surprises, but this is my home and where I lay my head at. If I just met you, would you like for me to pop up at your house unexpected?" I'm just being honest. We're not on that level to be doing pop ups.

"I feel where you're coming from but damn baby, I'm a gentleman and I'm trying to court you. I would never ask you out on a date and not pick you up from your door step. What type of shit is that? Excuse me for over stepping my boundaries."

"I appreciate you for being a gentleman. Come in so I can put these in some water." Malik took a seat on my sofa while I placed my flowers in a vase with some water.

After I locked up my loft, Malik grabbed my hand and escorted me to his car. Damn, he was different. I can get used to this. He opened the door for me and didn't close it until I had my seat belt fastened.

"So, tell me a little bit about yourself, Leah. Why are you single?" Damn, he's digging deep. I'm not ready to open up about my break up with Vell. It is what it is.

"Do you care Malik or you're just being nosey?"

"I care Leah or else I wouldn't have asked you. I could give two fucks about the next man. I'm on the outside looking in. You're a diamond baby. I just want to polish you. I can see the dimness. I just want to shine some light on you."

"I appreciate that Malik. We were engaged to be married. I was planning our wedding. He cheated with a chick that smiled up in my face on the daily, so I let him go. Is there anything else that you want to know?"

"Damn baby, I'm sorry that shit happened to you. Sometimes BOYS get caught up. There's a difference between a boy and man. A real man would never play his woman like that. I'm just saying that's a little too close to home for me. I'm never risking home for some easy pussy. On some real shit, if any of my woman so-called friends would've been on some shit like that. I would've told my woman out the gate.

Excuse my language but a shiesty bitch like that will never have the upper hand on my woman. To each its own. That's just my perspective. I wouldn't want my woman to fuck a nigga that smiles up in my face. If one of my niggas ever played me that close, I swear its lights off and mask on." Damn, I felt all that.

"All men talk a good game if they're not the one in the situation. Actions speak louder than words. I don't care how good you put words together. Show me, don't tell me nothing."

"I feel you, lil baby. I don't have to put on or gloat about me. I don't have a problem showing you the real me, if you would allow me too." I wish he would stop looking at me when he talks.

"We'll see."

"I'll take that." Malik and I continued our conversation. I enjoyed his conversation, but you would have to do more than talk to me. You would have to show me. Talk is cheap.

Malik and I finally made it to our destination, Top Golf. It was lit for a Tuesday. I saw Alonzo's car in the parking lot. Just my luck to run into his crazy ass. I shot Alexis a text to see if she was inside. She said no. I asked her was Vell with Alonzo she said she didn't think so. Just my luck when I decide to take Malik up on his offer for a date, I run into somebody that I don't want to see. Malik found us a parking spot. When I attempted to open the door, he swatted at my hand.

"I got it. Stay put until I let you out." He chuckled. I did as I was told. He was a real gentleman. He opened the door for me. We held hands as we walked in. As soon as we hit the entrance all eyes were on us. Damn, he must come here a lot.

"Mr. Devereaux your host will be right with the two of you," the greeter stated. I knew he was too good to be true. He probably takes everybody here. A date, nigga please. Hood niggas don't date. I should walk off from his ass and call me an Uber back home. Ole girl knew his last name.

"Ms. Lady say what you need to say. Don't ever bite your tongue." He explained. I cocked my neck to the side and turned my face up. As far as I'm concerned what's understood doesn't need to be explained.

"Do I need to say something Malik? If so, let me know so I can show my ass up in this motherfucka." I argued and sassed. I bet he wasn't expecting that. Malik stepped all in my personal space. He whispered in my ear, where only I could hear. I felt a few chills run through my body.

"I wish you would show your motherfuckin ass up in here. I ain't that nigga Ms. Lady. I'm the district manager in this motherfucka. I'll escort you right to my office and fuck the shit out of you. You need the right man to tame you. I'm going to calm all of that down. How much you want to fuckin' bet?" I just came on myself. I need to use the bathroom and toss this thong in the trash.

"Excuse me I need to use the bathroom." I had to get the fuck away from him.

"You're excused." He whispered in my ear. "I got that pussy wetter than a motherfucka huh?" I ignored him and walked fast as I could to the bathroom. I bumped into Alonzo on the way. I wasn't about to admit to that.

"Damn Leah, what's up? Who are you up in here with?" He asked. Damn, I could've sworn my father was in the FEDS doing life in prison for murder. I don't know why he wanted to hit me with these twenty-one questions.

"What's up Zo. I'm with an associate, why?" I argued. I'm trying to trash these thongs and get back to my date.

"Where is she?" He asked. I walked in the bathroom. I don't have to answer to Alonzo when Vell was cheating. He wasn't telling that nigga to stop cheating. I can't believe I'm coming up out of my thong in this stall. Thank God I had some wipes in my purse. I should've kept my ass at home. I checked my face to make sure I was good. As soon as I stepped out the bathroom Alonzo was still out there. I swear if he called Vell I'm going off.

"What Zo, shouldn't you be heading home to Alexis? Mind your business and not mine."

"You are my business if my OG isn't in attendance. You know I owe you one because you set me up at Zone 6 Day. The only reason I'm not calling him is because I can't let my OG catch a case that's not in our jurisdiction. You know that nigga is living in his last days fuckin' with you." He threatened. I swear I can't stand Alonzo, and Vell always wants to kill somebody. Just take that fuckin' L. Women take them all the time.

"Whatever Zo let me go enjoy my date. I'm single and Vell is too. Find Vell a bitch okay and be glad Alexis took your ass back. You don't owe me shit but a thank you." I argued. I walked off from Alonzo. He was killing my vibe. As soon as I hit the corner Malik was waiting for me.

"What's wrong Ms. Lady?" He asked.

"Nothing." I sassed. I couldn't tell Malik about the exchange Alonzo and I had. I shot Alexis a text and told her to get her man and don't give his ass any pussy or head since he's a snitch.

"Ms. Lady don't start fuckin' lying to me. Let's be honest with each other. I'm not trying to gain anything by lying to you."

"I ran into my EX'S right-hand man. We had a few words. It's my business and not yours." Malik reached for my hand and led me to our section. I was hungry so of course, I wanted to eat before I beat his ass in golf. Malik and I ordered our food. He had the table setup nice. I guess it's a perk being the district manager. I just knew he was a real dope boy. He reached over the table and grabbed my hands.

"Your hands are soft. The only thing missing is a glacier on your left hand. Why are you so quiet? Talk to me. I'm trying to get to know you, Ms. Lady." Our host came and took our order. I only wanted appetizers. Malik was making me uncomfortable staring at me.

"What do you want to talk about Malik?" I sighed. He was so manly that it's crazy to me.

"You. I hope I didn't offend you earlier. On some real shit Ms. Lady, you didn't deserve any of the shit you went through. My sister went through some similar shit a few months ago. It hit close to home when you revealed that. It took a minute for her to bounce back." He explained.

"Thank God she has a brother like you in her corner to make sure she's good."

"She's my little sister. It's my job to make sure she's straight. Who's in your corner to make sure you're straight Leah?"

"I don't have anybody in my corner. I know if nobody doesn't have my back. I got my own back."

"I hear you Ms. Lady, but everybody needs somebody. This world wasn't made for us to be alone. It's somebody for everybody."

"I hear you, but why don't you have anybody? On the outside looking in you seem like a great guy? Why are you single? Who's in your corner? Why don't you have a ring on your finger?"

"I'm ready to settle down. I'm faithful. I want a wife. I want to get married. I want to share my wealth. I work a lot, but that's just an excuse. I haven't found the right one worthy enough to carry my last name. I've run across a lot of women in my day, but they only want two things from me and that's this dick and my bag. If I'm not here handling business for these locations, then I'm handling business that I oversee."

"How do you know you haven't found the right one?"

"I know I haven't Leah because if I did, I wouldn't have asked you out. I would be at home cooking and catering to my wife." Saved by the food. I guess he told me. Malik and I started eating our food. We didn't talk much, but we stole a few glances at each other. He has me speechless. I can't lie, I'm feeling some type of way. I felt a chill run through me. I wish my grandmother was here. It felt like he was talking to my soul instead of just casual conversation. After finishing our food, Malik grabbed my hand and led the way to the golf course.

"Do you know how to play Leah, or do I have to teach you? I want to teach you a few things," he chuckled.

Malik thought he was slick, but he couldn't run game on me.

"I know how to play." Yeah, I snagged a few golfers in my day at East Lake Golf Course. I couldn't go there without knowing how to play.

"Okay you can go first," he stated. I know I can, ladies always go first. I grabbed the golf puck and attempted to swing. I heard Malik laugh. I stopped what I was doing and turned around to see what was so funny. He knew I was about to light fire in his ass. He plays too much.

"What's so funny?" I asked. I rested the golf puck in my free hand.

"You, let me show you how to do this shit the right way." He chuckled. Malik walked up behind me. Damn, he smelled good. I inhaled his cologne. He wrapped his hands around my waist. He rested his chin in the nape of my neck. He was trying to get close to me by using teaching me how to play golf as an excuse.

"You smell good Ms. Lady."

"Tell me something I don't know. Look don't be trying to get free feels and shit. Teach me how to play or back the fuck up." I argued. He grabbed a hand full of my ass. I swatted his hands, none of that. If I grabbed his dick, he'll be feeling some type of way.

"Leah, where are your panties?" He asked? Why is he worried about my panties? I trashed them motherfuckas over forty-five minutes ago.

"Malik, let's play golf okay." I tried to ignore his question. What I do is my business we're not together.

"I need you to answer my question because when you sat down in my ride. I saw the string of your thong holding on to your ass for dear life and I don't see that shit anymore." He argued. Damn, he noticed all of that? He was paying attention to detail. I should've worn a belt. I picked up a few pounds because it's the winter and I've been in the house cooking all types of shit. I like the extra pounds. I've always been a thick girl. I wouldn't have it any other way.

"They were making me uncomfortable, so I took them off and trashed them." Malik looked at me. He knew I was lying. Shit, I came all on myself. My pussy was to wet to be walking around with those thongs on. He had my pussy doing flips.

"Yeah, that better be the fucking' case." Malik finally got serious and started teaching me how to play golf. We were laughing and having a good time. I beat his ass like I knew I would. I enjoyed this, it was different.

Alonzo and two of his niggas walked passed us. He held up his phone. I knew he was on live so Vell could see. The worse thing Alonzo messy ass could do was provoke me. I'm trying to be on my best behavior but it's niggas like him that'll make me show the fuck out. I'm not trying to get Malik caught up in my shit.

"Aye Leah playing Golf with another nigga that's not my nigga don't look good on you. I see you though." He argued. He just had to say something. I flipped his ass two birds and it's literally fuck him. Malik busted out laughing. I joined him. Alonzo was funny as hell. He didn't like that shit at all. Malik and I enjoyed our night. This was a cool first date. We rode through the city blowing on some real fruity shit. Sirius XM was blaring through his speakers. It fucked me up when **Can't You See by Total** came on. I know I couldn't sing but fuck it that was my song. I had to hit that chorus one time. I'll blame it on the weed and alcohol.

I can't wait for the day that we can be together

I can't let you walk away can't you see you and me

Were meant to be, oh baby and there's nothing left to say

If that wasn't a sign. Malik and I were nodding our heads to the music. You couldn't tell me I wasn't Kisha from Total back in the day. It's the beginning of winter so of course, it's cold. The heat was blasting too. It felt good to be in the presence of a grown ass man. I could tell he had his shit together and that's a bonus. I wasn't ready to go home yet when Malik pulled up to my loft.

"Can I walk you to your door or is that a problem?" He asked. Malik got me feeling his ass just a little bit. He could walk me to my door. I'll fuck with him and say no just to get his blood pumping.

"I'm good Malik. I got it from here." I was just fuckin' with him to see what he would say. I notice he gripped his steering wheel.

"Alright, Ms. Lady." He sighed.

"Come on Malik you can walk me to my door." I laughed.

"You play too much."

"I know." Malik grabbed my hand. It was freezing cold. We finally made it to my loft and unlocked my door. "Thank you for taking me out tonight. It was fun."

"I enjoyed your company Ms. Lady, maybe we can do it again one day."

"Maybe." Malik pulled me in his arms for a bear hug. I wrapped my arms around his neck and he lifted my legs around his waist. We just smiled at each other. He bit his bottom lip and I gave him a peck on his lips.

"You know I don't want to put you down. I like this. I'm feeling you, Leah. I want to see you tomorrow if that's cool."

"I don't want you to put me down either and you can definitely see me tomorrow." Malik freed my legs from around his waist. He kissed me and made sure I locked the door behind me. I slid down the crease of my door in the dark smiling. The light in my living room flicked on and it was Vell.

Chapter 6

Vell

"OG Vell. Aye man I'm at Top Golf handling some business. Your old lady up in here with another man. I feel like making my fuckin' presence known. You want me to handle this shit? I got eyes on this nigga and I can have this bitch surrounded in less two minutes. Give me the okay and I'm setting this bitch off like it's New Year's around this bitch." My nigga Zo was always on go. Leah know what it is with me, she knows how I give it up. She knows I'll pull up.

"Good looking Zo, you know I like to get my hands dirty myself. I got it though." I swear Leah is still on that bull shit. She ain't gone never forgive a nigga. I'm tired of this shit for real. I'm about to do something about it. I know I hurt her and I'm sorry as fuck that I did that shit. In my thirty-five years of living, I ain't never cared about a female the way I care about her. I never thought about settling down until I ran across her.

She got me out here in these streets looking like I damn fool. She won't even talk to a nigga. I learned my fuckin' lesson. Niggas change and I fuckin' changed. What the fuck am I supposed to do? All my niggas are tied down except for me. It's getting lonely out here in these streets. I want my lady back. That's all I want. I wish I could turn back the hands of time. I swear I wouldn't have fucked that bitch. Her loose ass pussy wasn't even worth it. I should've killed that bitch too.

Leah can't entertain another nigga period. She thought I didn't know where the fuck she laid her head at. I'm a killer, I can get in anywhere. I swear if she would've brought that nigga in here and gave up my pussy, I would've murdered that nigga right here. I was grilling the fuck out of her and she knows why I'm fuckin' here.

"Vell, why are you in my fuckin' house? You got to stop this shit. We aren't together, and I've made myself clear about that several times."

"Leah, I hear you, but I don't fuckin' hear you. We're on a break I'm coming back home and if it's a nigga in my way, then I'm moving him the fuck up out of my way. Don't fuckin' disrespect me by being out here on some lovey dovey shit. It took everything in me not to murk you and that nigga. I had that red beam on his ass when you unlocked the door.

Don't be out here giving niggas false hope. If you like that nigga and you want him to continue to live in the land of the living, you'll stop fuckin' with him or else I'll kill him. I could've had Alonzo to handle that shit, but I wanted to give you the warning myself."

"Vell, you can't be out here giving demands. We're not together. Do you think I want to be out here dating different niggas? I don't want to, but you forced my fuckin' hand. You caused all this, my nigga. You cheated on me. I'm trying to live my best life. I'm not going to stop living because of you. I refuse to do that. Why would you want to kill an innocent person because you fucked up? He doesn't have shit to do with me and you? If you got an issue take that shit up with yourself.

Vell, before I met you, I was running through niggas like that shit was going out of style. I changed because I thought we had some real shit going on. Silly me you turned out to be like the rest of these niggas. I'm growing with or without you. You can't stop the process my nigga. You Vell pushed me into the arms of another man. I didn't go because I wanted too. I'm so fuckin' tired of talking about this shit and addressing it. Let's just call this shit for what it is. I took a loss fuckin' with you Vell. Take your loss and leave me the fuck alone. I'm glad you care, but you didn't care enough to stop fuckin' that bitch when we made it official." She argued.

"Leah-" she cut me off quick.

"I don't want to hear it Vell, you know where the door is, you can let yourself out."

"Leah, I don't take losses. God can take me right now. If you think you can be with another nigga in my fuckin' city without any fuckin' repercussions, your sadly mistaken. It ain't going down like that. I'm not threatening you, that's a fuckin' promise.

Try me, Leah, if you want too. I dare you too. I ain't got nothing but time to kill any nigga that think they can get at you without being touched. You belong to me so stop playing with me. Get your black dress, because you'll be attending a lot of fuckin' funerals fuckin' with me. Trust me, it'll be some slow singing and flower bringing. Yeah, that's how I'm fuckin' coming. We gone get this shit right rather you like it or not." I argued.

"You can't force me to be with you Vell. I'll never force a nigga to be with me period."

"I haven't forced you to do anything yet, but I can, and I will." I walked up out Leah's. I had to get the fuck up out of there quick before I fuck around and hurt her ass. I sped out of her parking lot doing a fuckin' doughnut. I know she heard me. I grabbed my phone to call my little brother to see what's up with him. He answered on the first ring.

"What's up OG, what the fuck is going on with you this time of night? Do I need to pull up?" My brother already knew it was something if I was calling his ass this time of night.

"I'm getting ready to come through and holla at you for a minute before I get ready to hurt Leah's ass and wake Malone up too. I'm trying to see why she didn't tell me Leah was around town creeping with another nigga. I know she knew."

"Alright come through." He stated. This little bull shit me and Leah got going on ain't about nothing. Whoever this nigga is he better ask about me. I'm all about that gun play.

I pulled up at Sphinx's house and called him instead of ringing the doorbell. It was already late, and I wasn't trying to wake my nieces and nephews up, but I had to holla at my brother and get this shit off my chest. Sphinx opened the door and I followed him into the house. We headed to his man cave. He poured the two of us a shot. I took the shot to the head and slammed the shot glass on the table. Sphinx followed up behind me.

"What brings you by OG, what happened?" I gave Sphinx the rundown of what happened. He looked at me and shook his head. I'm not looking for an opinion. I'm looking for advice.

"OG Vell, Leah's a different breed. Some shit doesn't happen overnight. Give her space. If it's meant to be then let the cards fall where they're supposed too."

"Sphinx, how much space does she fuckin' need. Damn it's been six months already? I want to invade her space. Leah is ready to die. I've killed motherfuckas for less. I know we're not together in her eyes but in mine we are. It ain't no fuckin breaking up. Shit if I recall you didn't give Malone space." I argued.

"Look Vell, I'm going to keep shit ninety-five with you, that's all I can do. I know I've done my fair share of dirt. Settling down wasn't even in the cards for me. Shit, you know how I gave it up.

I ran across Malone and she made me want to say fuck all this shit because she didn't give in. She wasn't like everyone else. She could give two fucks about what I had and what I could offer her. In the beginning, I wasn't the best man to Malone and I could've been, but I was set in my ways.

I took advantage of her feelings and I shouldn't have. I didn't give her any space, but when the shit about Deja came out and Malone got cased up. I knew I had to get my shit together because when I got the call that she was in the county, my heart caved in because she was there because of me. Any other female would've sung like a bird.

I took her away from her shorty's. On some real shit, that hurt a niggas' soul. I knew I was in love with her, and I had to get my shit right. Our future wasn't looking bright, but it worked out. If you love Leah stay on her and don't ease the fuck up."

"I feel you. I shouldn't have done that shit. I fucked up, but I've learned my lesson. I'm not losing Leah. I don't take L's at all." I finished chopping it up with Sphinx. As soon as I was about to head out, I ran into Malone. I know she was ease dropping. She walked in grilling Sphinx

"What's up Vell? What are you doing here this time of night? Sphinx, why are you sneaking out of bed?" She argued and yawned.

"My bad Malone I had to holla at my brother before I kill your best friend and her new little boyfriend, she calls herself flexing with. Talk to Leah for me. I'm about to head out of here and take it in for the night." I slapped hands with Sphinx and kissed Malone on her cheek and headed out the door.

Chapter-7

Shon

"**B**end over LAYLA and ARCH that motherfuckin' back. Yeah right there. I love your little pretty brown ass face, down tussling with the pillows running from this dick. I like your fat ass sitting up, waiting on me to smack it," I moaned and grunted. I bit Layla's ear. I continued to pound Layla from the back. I was putting in overtime, while sweat was running down my chest and dripping between the crack of her ass. Her moans mixed with the sounds of how wet her pussy was, had me in a trance. Layla thought she was grown as fuck and in control. She looked over her shoulders and gave me a devilish grin mixed with fuck faces. I tried to avoid eye contact with her. I wasn't ready to bust a nut right now. She was making it real hard for me. I hate when she does that shit.

"Shon, I want you to FUCK me harder," she moaned. Layla knew that shit turned me on in the worst way. Alright, she'll fuck around and go in labor telling me to fuck her harder, and she'll be holding her stomach afterwards. She heard what the doctor said, she totally ignored that shit.

"You don't want that Layla. I promise you don't." Layla bit her bottom lip. She was a real freak. I knew she was up to something. She slithered her body like a snake and started grinding on my dick. I could feel her pussy muscles tighten. I was about to nut, and she was too. What little hair she had on her head, I wanted to rip that shit off. I grabbed both of her breasts and held on to them for dear life. She wanted to catch all of this.

I wrapped my hands around her throat and increased my death strokes to match her rhythm. Her eyes rolled in the back of her head. "Open your fuckin' eyes, Layla." She's been feeling okay lately. I know she's ready to give birth to our daughter Shalani Serenity Adams. My little princess is late. She's taking her precious time coming and I couldn't wait to meet her. I raised up to grab a towel to clean Layla and myself up. I ran downstairs to the kitchen to get Layla some grapes, yogurt and a water. I fed Layla a few grapes and a few spoons of yogurt.

"Shon, I'm tired and your daughter is stubborn just like you. I'm ready to get this over with and meet my princess," she pouted. My daughter was due to arrive yesterday, but she hasn't come yet. I needed Layla to be a little more patient. I think she was in a rush because Malone had her babies already. We needed this time alone. Who knows when we'll be able to do this again with a new baby in the picture.

"I know Layla she's coming, be patient. I'm sure she can't wait to meet you either." Layla scooted her body next to mine. I started massaging her shoulders and rubbing her stomach. Layla was fast asleep, sounding like a big ass grizzly bear. I couldn't wait to meet my princess. I would have two women to spoil.

If she's anything like her mother, my mother and sister, I'm done. She's going to have me wrapped around her finger. I can't wait to torture little boys who think they have a chance with my daughter. It's not fuckin' happening! Layla and I were both tired. We both dozed off to sleep. I had a few runs to make later, but fuck that a nigga was tired as fuck.

"Shon, wake up I think it's time. My stomach hurts so bad. I went to the bathroom and I saw a few specs of blood," she cried and yelled. I looked up at Layla and she was holding her stomach. I tried to warn her hard-headed ass earlier, but no she wanted me to fuck her harder. I didn't even realize I fell asleep that fast. I hope its time for our daughter. Hospitals are cool but nasty. I didn't want to stay at the hospital for two or three days, so they could look after my daughter. Our daughter will be born here right at home with Dr. Smith and our midwife Nurse Brooke. I had Layla a maternity room setup downstairs in our basement, where all our family and friends could be here.

"Layla, are the contractions coming close together or are they far apart?" I asked. Layla had us in every parenting and Lamaze class you could think of. I didn't mind doing it. I wanted to be the perfect father. My father was a real OG. I hope I could be half the man he was. I need a son and then I'll be complete

"SHON, they're coming close together. I don't think I can push this baby out," she yelled and screamed. She threw a baby bear at me. It's too late for this shit.

She better gets ready to start pushing our daughter out. She was just complaining about her not coming on time. Be careful what you wish for because you just might get it.

"Okay breathe Layla, let's call Dr. Smith and Nurse Brooke." I laughed. The fuck does she want me to do? It looks like today might be the day. "Get ready to prop those legs up and push, so we can make another one."

"It's not funny Shon. I called them already, they're on the way," she sassed. Layla has an attitude because she's in pain. I need the doctors to get here now before we have a fuckin' problem.

I called my mom, Shaolin, OG Lou, Malone, Dino, and Vell, they're on their way. My phone started ringing. I was hoping it was the doctor, but it was Sphinx and Vell on FaceTime. I swear I'm not beat for their shit today. My daughter is about to come in the world any minute now. I'll have to make sure everything is in place and Layla's straight.

"What's up Sphinx and Vell, are y'all on the way?" I asked. I could tell both of those niggas was higher than a giraffe's pussy.

I needed a bag of that good shit, fuckin' with Layla's crazy ass. I need that shit right now. I needed to get high as fuck before she has my daughter. She was already bitching.

"Hell, yeah we are on the way. Layla called us crying. I thought you beat her ass or some shit. I thought we were about to pull up on you and body your ass. I didn't know what the fuck was going on. She's still my baby even though she's older than me." he laughed. Sphinx was crazy as hell. I swear Layla and her tears will get somebody killed. I need her to toughen up because she'll be pregnant again real soon.

"Nigga get the fuck out of here with that shit. If you make my sister cry, I'll body your ass too. If she was crying, ain't shit you can do about it. She's about to push our daughter out any minute now. Bring me an ounce of that fruity shit y'all smoking on." I laughed. I finished chopping it up with Vell and Sphinx on FaceTime. They were fuckin' with my baby while she's in pain and she broke my phone. I know Shalani wasn't causing her that much pain? Layla just wanted to do that shit to prove a point. She wanted my attention and she had it.

"What you want me to do baby?"

"I want these fuckin' contractions to stop Shon. They hurt so fuckin' bad. I don't like the way this shit feels at all. Your daughter is punishing me." She wined. Layla was being real dramatic right now.

"Baby, if I could I would. You know I don't want you in any pain, that's just a part of the birth process. It'll be over soon." Layla wasn't trying to hear that at all.

Layla

I'm so fuckin' nervous my water finally broke fuckin' with Shon's ass. He's always trying to get some pussy. I was trying to get some dick too. It was felling so good in that moment. I knew better. I swear sex with Shon was so fuckin' amazing. It was like an outer body experience. The doctor told us to be careful while having sex, but we weren't listening as usual. Shon knew to take it easy on me. I guess Shalani said she was tired of us going at it like we didn't have any sense.

We got it in one good time. Who knows when we'll be able to do this again. I had to take a good shower. I couldn't deliver Shalani smelling like fresh sex, ain't no way. I couldn't wait to meet my daughter. She's been controlling my body for the last nine months. Hopefully, today will be her birthday, November 18th, 2018. I'm nervous as fuck. I paid attention to the parenting classes and it's time for the real thing.

Thank God I didn't have to leave our home. Shon's crazy ass had a maternity ward setup in our home, so I would be giving birth right here in front of all our family. I like that better than going to the actual hospital because when Malone had the twins, we all got put out as soon as visitation hours were over. I wanted our family to share this experience with us. My mom would be here in three hours coming from Haiti.

Our mid-wife and doctor had finally arrived. Leilani and her boo Lorenzo pulled up. Shon was about to stop him at the door. I swear he needs to get over it because his mother is dating again. My mother face-time me and told me do not have her grand-daughter if she wasn't here. I intended to do just that. I pray Shalani doesn't come until she arrives. Malone and Sphinx arrived. Linda Faye and OG Lou were already here. Vell pulled up and Leah was right behind him. I looked out the window and saw him waiting on her. Shon grabbed my hand and led me in the kitchen and told me to stop being nosey. I just wanted my brother and Leah back together.

"Come on Layla are you ready? I need you to get off your feet and relax, so you can prepare for our daughter to come." He explained. Shon always knows how to ruin shit. He knew I was nosey as fuck. It's getting close to the holidays and I wanted everybody to be in the spirit.

"I'm ready Mr. Adams." Shon carried me to our maternity ward. Dr. Smith and Nurse Brook were setting the room up, so they could prep us for delivery. Shon helped me undress. I had a cute Victoria Secrets night gown that I was wearing. Shon looked at me and bit his bottom lip. Having a maternity ward in our home was a perk. I was slaying for this delivery. Malone was our photographer. She would be taking my pictures.

I pulled the gown over my head and Shon pulled my panties down and held them by his nose. "Damn that pussy smells good." He laughed. Shon stuffed them in his pants, I swear he does the most. Shon and I walked out and joined the rest of the family. I could smell the food cooking. OG Lou, Leilani, and Linda Faye were upstairs doing their thing. I walked my ass straight up there. I knew I wasn't supposed to eat anything, but I had to try my luck. I tried to grab a piece of the chicken.

"Layla you know you can't eat this. Shon give her some ice and some hard candy." She argued. OG Lou popped me on my hand. I pouted. Ugh, it's too bad I couldn't eat anything until after I had her. I'm starving, and this food aroma is driving me insane. I headed back downstairs to kick it with Malone and Leah.

"Layla, you look so beautiful. I'm jealous as fuck. When I was pregnant why didn't you suggest that I get a maternity ward built or you could've offered me to use yours? Your maternity photos are popping. Sphinx, I need one of these before I give you any more babies." She beamed. I love the way Sphinx looks at Malone. She ain't talking about nothing with her fertile ass. The only thing she was pushing out was twins. Sphinx wanted a big family. He'll do whatever for her to make sure she's happy.

"Sis, awe thank you. You know your husband will make it happen. I looked at Sphinx, he looked at me and nodded his head at me in agreeance. Leah, you're up next. I want a niece from you and Vell." I laughed. I meant that shit too because Vell needed a child to calm him down. I can't believe he doesn't have any children running around out here yet. Leah gave me a look that could kill. Vell was smiling, but he needs to pray because it isn't looking so good for him.

"Dr. Williams please give her an epidural or some type of pain medication. Clearly, she's losing her mind" She laughed. Everybody was laughing except for Vell. He didn't think that shit was funny at all. "Layla, please don't do that." Malone, Leah and I sat back, talked, and took a shit load of pictures. The contractions were starting to speed up. My mother called and said she was forty-five minutes away. Thank God because I don't how much longer I could wait.

My nurse and mid-wife came in and started hooking the IV's up to me. They checked my blood pressure and my iron. Everything was fine so far. I was getting tired again. Shon came into the room and climbed in the bed beside me. He wrapped his hands around my stomach and he rested his chin on the crook of my neck. Shalani was being her usual self. She started moving around, she knew when her father was near. I turned around to face Shon and he cupped my face, while I stroked his beard. I love this man. I gave him a quick peck on his lips and he grabbed the back of my head and started tonguing me down. This is exactly how Shalani got here nine months ago. Nurse Brook came in to check and see how many centimeters I was.

"Six centimeters Mrs. Adams." She beamed. Shalani would be here in no time. I couldn't wait to meet her. I know she's going to be beautiful. Shon was stroking the side of my face looking at me.

"Are you ready to bring my daughter into the world?" He asked.

"Of course, I am. I've been waiting on this for weeks." I could get lost in Shon's eyes. I swear he's everything to me.

"Layla, I made it. Let's do this. Shon back up off my baby. You're the reason she's here in the first place," my mother laughed. I'm glad she finally made it. My mother is a nurse too. She had to be here to help deliver her granddaughter. My mother changed into her scrubs.

"She's my baby too, you know I love her." He chuckled. Dr. Smith and Nurse Brook came in to check me one more time. Hopefully, Shalani is ready since her grandmother was here.

"Mrs. Adams, you're at nine centimeters. Let's get you prepped for delivery, so you can meet your daughter soon." Thank God, I couldn't wait to meet her.

Shon looked at me. I was nervous again, and I don't know why. He was right by my side and hasn't left. I started sweating and he grabbed a cold towel to wipe my face because I was hot. Then he held my hand for reassurance.

"Come on Baby, we got this. I got you, I'm not going anywhere." He stated. Shon placed a kiss on my lips. It was time to get this delivery started. I closed my eyes and said a quick prayer.

"Mrs. Adams on the count of three push for me. 1,2,3." I started to push. Nurse Brook instructed me to push again. I started pushing too early. "Come on Layla, you can do better than that," my mother yelled. Not now momma.

"I'm trying," I whined. I prayed I didn't shit while Shon was here. It felt like I had to shit bad too.

"Layla, don't push unless we tell you too." My mother warned me.

"One more push." Dr. Williams and Nurse Brooked yelled. "I see hair, she has a head full." No wonder I had heart burn so bad. I had to push one more time. Come on

Shalani don't make mommy work so hard. She's stubborn just like Shon and Malone. She wasn't ready to come out yet. I pushed again and screamed. I'm never having another child again. "She's coming." My mother yelled. Thank God. I don't think I had another push in me.

My daughter came out screaming. She had a set of lungs on her. She weighed in at eight pounds and two ounces. She was screaming as loud as she could too. She was a hell raiser. She was so pale. I couldn't wait for her to get some color. She looks like a little mouse.

Shon cut her umbilical cord, then my doctor and midwife started cleaning me up. It was blood everywhere. I haven't had a cycle in months and I wasn't looking forward to one. I'm ready to hold my daughter and eat a hot meal. My mother cleaned Shalani up and handed her to me. She was so beautiful. I couldn't stop looking at her.

"Can I see me my baby Layla?" I handed Shalani to her father. As soon as she heard his voice. I could've sworn I saw her crack a smile. Shalani looks nothing like me, but like her father. She only has my head, hair, chin, and dimples. She's beautiful, she looks like a porcelain doll.

"Daddy did all the work." He laughed. I looked at Shon and rolled my eyes.

"He sure did, because he couldn't stay up out this pussy. He better make it count for something." My mother and nurse looked at us. I'm grown what did she expect, she walked in on him giving me head a few months ago.

"Layla, you didn't want me to stay up out of you." He chuckled and smirked.

"Yeah right. Whatever Shon. Shalani mommy rode the fuck out of daddy's dick." I laughed.

"Yeah because that's all you wanted me to do, was ride this dick."

"No that's what you wanted me to do."

"I can't wait for you to get back up there and ride it again." He laughed.

"Wait on it, Shon! Are you shitting me! I'm not riding any dick for a few months."

"Is that what you think? I heard I had to wait six weeks, not a few months?" He asked. I wasn't even about to respond to him. Shon got me fucked up. I don't know who told him six weeks. That was my business and not his. I know Shon, and I refuse to let him put any more voodoo on my pussy. I'm not trying to make another baby anytime soon. I'm trying to snap back. It's the winter time too. I'm ready to suit up. Shon was looking at me and I refuse to give him any eye contact. I wanted a son, but we need to be married first and Shalani needs to be at least a year or two years old before we do that. He can cum anywhere but inside of me.

"Layla, thank you for giving birth to my daughter. I love you and I'll do anything in this world to make you and her happy." He stated. Shon cupped my face and placed a wet kiss on my lips. Shalani started crying. It's a little too early to be a cock blocker.

"I love you too."

Chapter-8

OG Lou

I wish Leilani would bring her ass on. It's almost 3:00 p.m. I've called her at least four times already and she hasn't answered the fuckin phone one time. She should've been here over an hour ago and she only lives less than twenty minutes away. Ever since she's started riding a new dick, I can't get her to handle business like she needs too. I need to get to the store before it closes. I don't have time to be at the store all day. I close my trap down every day for an hour and forty-five minutes to handle my fuckin' business. I called Day and he's not answering his fuckin' phone either. I know one thing, he better not bring his ass here tonight to lay his fuckin' head. My house ain't the fuckin' crash spot. Get your own shit. Chanta thinks she slick, and Day is too dumb to see it. She's only using him for dick, nothing more nothing less.

I refuse to be in the kitchen all night cooking this Thanksgiving food. I don't know why they wanted to have that shit at my house anyway? Shon and Dino thought they were slick too. They wanted to post up at my spot to get rid of some of their work for free. Not fuckin' happening. They have to pay me to fuckin' move that shit over here. It's a consignment fee. Shon knows he can't run game on me. I heard my door open and it was finally Leilani's ass, about fuckin' time.

"Hey, momma! Sorry I'm late, are you ready to go? It smells good in here already." She beamed, sorry my ass. Leilani was a little to chipper for a motherfucka this late. She must have just gotten some dick.

"Leilani don't hey momma me. It's about time you decided to show your face. It'll smell better if I had all the food. I'd be half way done by now. Come on, let's go because I got shit to do." I argued. I'm on one. Leilani knows I hate to be late or running behind schedule.

"Momma you ain't the only one that got something to do." She argued. If she had something to do, she should've done it already. It took everything in me not to smack fire from her ass. She's on my time, it's not the other way around.

"Leilani Serenity Adams shut up, don't fuckin' start with me today. You already fuckin' late. If you want to have Thanksgiving at your house this year, we can by all fuckin' means. I ain't got to cook none of this shit. My hands are reserved for whipping work. I can chill on some real OG shit. Ever since you got a new dick stroking your cat, you act like you're losing your fuckin' mind." I argued. I placed my hand on my hip and grilled Leilani. I didn't even grab my coat or purse. I wanted her to see I wasn't playing today. I wasn't in the mood. She can pack up all this food and take it to her house to cook."

"Momma, what's wrong with you? I was only a few minutes late. Dick will never be the reason why I can't handle my business. I can't believe you tried me like that. Come on let's go I'm in the same business you're in. Malone said she'll make the potato salad." She stated. I know she didn't say what the fuck I thought she said. I'm about to check her right now. Malone isn't about to fuck up my dinner with her potato salad.

"Leilani I'mma tell you just like I'm going to tell your daughter. I don't give a DAMN who feelings I hurt. If she brings that dry ass potato salad in here this Thanksgiving I'm going to snap. Do you fuckin' hear me? I don't give two fucks about her being married to a damn

Trap God. I was married to one too. Sphinx knows that shit was nasty as hell. He trashed that shit at the Fourth Of July Barbecue. I watched him do it, pussy whipped ass.

I'm not scared of Malone nor will I pacify her feelings. Shit, she worked at Publix for years. Her bougie ass could've bought some instead of bringing hers for me to eat. Do you see how fine I am? Her potato salad almost killed me. What recipe is she fuckin' using? She needs to add a shit load of mustard to her potato salad, sweet pickles, paprika and cook the fucking potatoes longer. You name it, she fuckin' needs it.

I took that nasty ass shit to bingo last year because YOU said it was good. All dem old motherfuckas was laughing at OG Lou. I heard them motherfuckas whispering talking about don't eat that potato salad Lou made. Y'all got me fucked up. I knocked all they asses off in Bingo that night. As soon as they got on the bus, I gave them an edible and robbed the shit out of them. Trust me that was the last time they said anything about OG Lou.

I'm charging $10.00 a plate and no refills on the Kool aid or tea. If you want dessert, it's an extra $2.50. If you want a picture in my Trap, it's an extra $5.00. Oh, and if Sphinx brings all his kids, I'll give them a family discount of $100.00. Shit, they are paying TIP to post up at The Trap Museum, they gonna fuckin' pay me too. If you want to go live in my shit, it's an extra $25.00. If you want to play cards and win some money in my shit, it's $75.00 per game. If you plan on fuckin' in my shit, it's $250.00 and a $100.00 cleaning fee. Guess what, Chanta and Day owe me some fuckin' money.

Chanta can't clean my fuckin' chitlins right because she's running up behind Day. Every time I look up my chitlins are just sitting in the sink not being cleaned. I don't give a fuck if she doesn't like them or not, you gone help clean them or take Day back with you wherever the fuck home is. I'm tired of him cock blocking when an OG is trying to holla at me. I wish he take his ass on."

"Momma, no offense but don't talk about my daughter like that. Just because her potato salad isn't up to your liking doesn't mean anything. Malone cooks healthy, she doesn't use all that unhealthy ass shit." She argued.

"Leilani, I don't give two fucks about how healthy she cooks. If it doesn't taste good, all that unhealthy shit goes out the window. I'm your OG Leilani, so who in the fuck are you talking too like that? Her husband doesn't fuckin'' like it, but I got to like it? He's too fuckin' scared to say something. I don't give a damn. I didn't like that nasty dry ass shit, period. She needed to add some unhealthy shit to it.

Since when you start pacifying a motherfucka feeling? See, that's your problem now, always pacifying your kids. I told you to raise Malone how I raised you, but nope you thought she was a princess. Which she is yours. If you would've taught her how to cook dope instead of letting her play with dolls, we wouldn't even be having this conversation."

"Momma come on, you're tripping for real. Malone cooks one thing that you don't like and we're having a full-blown argument about it? It's the holidays. I'm not trying to argue or be at odds with you. Call Malone and tell her don't make the potato salad since it's a problem."

She explained. I ain't got to tell Malone shit. She better have; a talk with her daughter her damn self; if she doesn't want me to put her ass on blast tomorrow. We finally left the house and made it to the store.

Leilani was too busy on her fuckin' phone to make sure I had everything I needed. I should've driven myself. You know what I refuse to let this child of mine worry me. It ain't happening. I checked my list twice to make sure I didn't forget anything. This was my last trip to the store. If I forgot it or was missing something. It wasn't getting cooked.

I finally made it back home. Kroger's and Publix were both at capacity. The police were outside directing traffic. I don't fuck with the police period. It was time for me to go. The police would take one look at me and swore I had warrants and shit. Anything to look me up. Leilani wanted to stop and talk to everybody she fuckin' saw. She went her way and I went mine.

I finished cleaning my chitlins that Chanta didn't fuckin' clean. I had to check them twice. I knew she half cleaned my shit. I peeled my onions and potatoes to kill the smell of the chitlins. I seasoned them with Lowry's Garlic salt, some Creole seasoning, and I added a little hot sauce. The aroma was smelling good. I bet you Day better not even have his hand out or a fork full. I jerked my ham, wrapped it in foil, and placed it in the oven. Then I seasoned and buttered my turkey and placed it in the oven.

My stuffing was prepped and ready to be put in the oven. The baked macaroni and cheese was finished. My greens and turkey necks were cooking and starting to smell good. Sweet potato soufflé was finished, so I topped it with marshmallows and pecans. My desserts were almost done also. I made my filling for the apple pie. I just had to seal it with the pie crust. I was finished the Banana Pudding already. I'm tired. I'm not cooking for Christmas. I know one thing, they better have their asses over at my house early to eat because after 7:00 p.m. they got to clear my shit. Our Thanksgiving food was finished and damn near ready to eat for tomorrow. It was time for me to lay it down. I cooked to damn much today. I wanted to have me a drink tonight.

As soon as I started to get some real rest, it was time to get up again. I swore I just closed my eyes. I looked at the clock and it was 11:26 a.m. I heard people already in my fuckin' house. I told Leilani about having motherfuckas in my trap if I wasn't up. She wanted to be on time today because she knew it was time to eat. Just like a damn nigga to be on time when it's time to eat. I heard my room door open and it was Leilani and Linda Faye.

"Who's in my house while I'm sleeping Leilani and Linda Faye?" I yawned.

"Good Morning to you too. Happy Thanksgiving ma. It's just us. We're setting up everything, so you don't have too. I know you stayed up all night and cooked. We appreciate you. Go ahead and take a shower. Oh, and Ma some man stopped by and dropped some flowers and two wads full of cash. He said he'll back later. He said his name was Earl Lee." She stated. Leilani was to fuckin' nosey. I'm the only one taking names around here.

"Leilani and Linda Faye ain't shit changed. Don't open my fuckin' door for niggas y'all don't know. You could've given Earl Lee those fuckin' ugly ass flowers back and kept the cash. Give it to me so I can count it," I argued. Linda Faye dumped the money on the floor, so I could count it later. Leilani looked at me and smiled on her way out the door. Earl Lee Roberts is finally out of jail after serving twenty-two years for robbing a Brinks truck. I heard he was getting out. I don't know why his first stop was my house. I'm glad that nigga dropped off a bag. Can't no nigga walk around owing OG Lou shit.

I needed my money. He owed it to me for not telling where the fuck his stash was at. I grabbed the money off the floor and counted it. It was only $10,000.00, he owes me ten more. I guess that was his reason to come back to drop that off. It was getting late. I had to get myself together. I grabbed a pair of Chanel Jeans and a Red Chanel sweater out of my closet.

The Dominicans gave me a blow out yesterday. I jumped in the shower and handled my hygiene. I was running low on the Thousand Wishes body wash, it's time to stack up. I could've sworn I stocked up on this body wash. I hate Bath and Body Works Christmas scents. I always stock up in the summer, so by the time I wouldn't need any more until Spring or Summer.

I dried my body off good. I made my face up with a light beat. I applied my Rihanna red stunna lips. I moisturized my body with the Thousand Wishes lotion. I took my scarf off and my hair fell to my back, while I ran a comb through it. It looked good. I slid my feet into my black Red Bottom Pumps. OG Lou was popping to be 62

BITCH GOOD BLACK DON'T CRACK. Everybody was starting to come. It was a little after 1:00 p.m., Shon, Layla, and the baby were one of the first ones to arrive. I stopped Shon right at the fuckin door. I had my hand out.

"Shon, it's $20.00 for you and Layla to get in." I laughed. He looked at me like I was crazy. I meant that shit. He already knew what time it was. I couldn't give Shon a pass because he would always expect a deal or something free. I taught him at an early age to pay as he weighs. Ain't nothing free in this world, not even the air he breathes.

"Come on OG Lou, damn we got to pay you to eat for Thanksgiving? You real petty for this shit. You always charging me for something." He chuckled. Hell yeah, he must pay. He didn't put in on the food or drinks. Shon pulled out a $20.00 bill from his bank roll. He better be glad I didn't charge for the baby. Sphinx and Malone were pulling up right behind them. Malone had a big bowl in her hand. I pray to God it's not that fuckin' potato salad. She tried to push past me without paying. I stopped her pretty ass right at the door.

"Grandma Lou I need to put this potato salad in the refrigerator." She beamed.

"It's OG Lou and you need to pay before you enter. It's a $100.00 entrance for you and your family. I'll have a talk with you later about this potato salad." I laughed. Malone looked at me like she had an attitude. She knew I wasn't bull shitting and she couldn't run game on me like she did her mother. Pay me or take your ass home.

"Grandma are you serious? Why do we have to pay? That's a lot of money to eat Thanksgiving food." She asked. She had her hands on her hips as if I were supposed to budge. Sphinx got it, she'll never go broke. I can vouch for him.

"I'm dead ass serious. This food ain't free and nor did you help cook it." Sphinx walked up behind Malone with the two car seats and pulled out $200.00 and handed them to me. Then he kissed me on my cheek. Malone was mad about that. Sphinx was my type of nigga.

He always paid without a problem. Vell was right behind them and he had a bitch with him. I gave him a look that could kill. He knew I wasn't cool with that shit. I don't know what type of shit he's on, but he doesn't want any problems here. He handed me a $20.00 bill for him and his chick. Leah walked up right behind him with Dino and Tory. I didn't make Leah pay.

Majority of our family has arrived. Malone, Layla, and Leah were putting up the Christmas tree. Leilani and Linda Faye were setting the table. I grabbed my camera to snap a few pictures. I haven't had a turn out like this in a long time. Damn, I have a beautiful family.

Last year around this time it was just Malone and her two children. This year it's a few new editions. She's married with a family. It's the same for Shon, he was by himself and now he's with Layla and they share a child. Even Leilani got her groove back. About fuckin' time. I would've been hopped on some new dick a few months after Big Shon died. Even Day got Chanta back. Jah and Samaya said they were hungry and ready to eat.

"Come on y'all let's eat, these kids are hungry." The kids sat at the smaller table and the adults were at the larger table. I poured me a glass of wine, shit was about to get interesting. Vell's little friend kept looking at Leah and smiling. See, females need to know their place, if a woman ain't checking for you don't check for her. Leah was better than me because, in my day, I'll slide a bitch. These hands quick and the fuck nigga sitting next to her too. Leilani decided to say grace. Leah sat by me and I cut my eyes at Vell. He tried so hard not to look at me. He knew he was wrong for bringing a bitch here in my shit to eat, just to fuck with Leah. Now he'll be mad if we set this bitch off. I elbowed Leah. She looked at me and smiled. She knew I was on my good bullshit. Don't fuck with my babies', period. Selfish ass bastard

"Do you want me to make her leave? I will and I ain't fuckin' whispering because this is MY SHIT and I'LL TALK RECKLESS AS FUCK. AIN'T NO BITCH COME BEFORE YOU?" Ole girl was looking at me. Vell held his head down. "Yes, lil girl, I'm talking about your ass. It ain't no secrets up in here." I argued.

"I'm SORRY I didn't mean to ruffle any feathers. Let me introduce myself. I'm Anissa. I'll leave. I'm not trying to make anybody uncomfortable," she stated. Sit down with that fake ass apology. She knew all about Leah. Leah and Malone were about to interrupt her. I had to cut in and interrupt them because I got this.

"Oh baby, you definitely can leave. Make no fuckin' mistake about it, you can roll the fuck up out of here. One more thing Anissa before you leave, you can never ruffle any feathers up in here. It's only one bird here in this room living and it's you. I cook birds for dinner. As you can see them motherfuckas laid on the table real pretty. You can never make Leah feel uncomfortable because this is her home too.

The only person that'll feel uncomfortable is you because Vell and Leah have history. I'm sure you can feel the tension between the two of them in the room. It's a family affair and I'm not sure why he invited you here. Whatever y'all got going on don't fall too hard because it's temporary. Take it from me he's just waiting on Leah to give him the okay." Malone and Layla started laughing, but I was dead ass serious.

"No, you can stay. OG Lou, she can stay she doesn't have to leave because of me. I'm not checking for Vell. He's all checked out." She laughed and stated. Leah was better than me because this bitch would have to get to stepping or else, I would step on her. Leilani went ahead and started with saying grace.

"God is good, and God is great all the time. Let us thank Him for our food. By His blessings we are fed, Give us Lord, our daily bread. Thank you, Lord, for everything that you have done in our life thus far. Thank you for these gifts which we are about to receive. Through Thy bounty Through Christ our Lord we pray. Amen." I thought Leilani was never going to get finished praying. My stomach was growling and damn near touching my back. I was hungry.

I fixed my plate and went into the kitchen to eat. I didn't need anybody in my face while I was eating. I noticed somebody walked up. I looked up and it was Sphinx and Malone. I wiped my mouth to see what was up. Malone knows I hate to be interrupted while I'm eating.

"Grandma I want you to taste my potato salad," she beamed and smiled. Sphinx was standing right behind her with a big smile on his face. They got me fucked up. I'm not with this tag teaming shit.

"I told you about that grandma shit. Its OG motherfuckin' Lou. I'm good Malone, I don't want any. Sphinx have you had some," I laughed and asked?

"Yeah OG I had some." He chuckled. I knew he was lying, they can't fuckin' try me like this. I'm too fly, to die. Malone is trying to take her OG out early.

"Come on Grandma. My momma told me you were talking about my potato salad? Sphinx helped me with this one." She beamed. Just because Sphinx helped doesn't mean shit. Hell, he probably can't cook.

"Malone, anything I say once I can for damn sure say it twice. I sure the fuck was talking about you and your potato salad, your husband was talking about it too. Always remember your OG Lou going to keep it real with you. I'll try a fork full of it that's it. I hope it's good or else I'll be checking the two of you and I'm going to beat your ass for making me try it. I ain't got nothing but time today." I grabbed a fork full. Umm, it tastes good unbelievably. I tried a little bit more.

"It's really good, y'all did that. Malone, why did the two of you walk up on me like y'all were about to check me? I don't like that shit. Don't roll up on me like that," I asked. The potato salad was good. It tastes a whole lot better than last time. Malone hid behind Sphinx. Shit, I'm not scared of his ass. He better asks about OG Lou.

"I couldn't have you out here talking about my wife." He chuckled.

"I wouldn't have to if you would've helped her out the last time." I took a few pictures of Sphinx and Malone. They looked good together. I knew this would happen months ago. Leilani and I placed a bet on this. Guess what, Leilani paid the fuck up. Malone knew she wanted him. She could never deny it. Linda Faye was passing out Jell-O shots. Vell came in the kitchen and got two. He rolled up some weed trying to avoid eye contact with me.

"What's up Vell?"

"Nothing much OG Lou, what you got going on?" He chuckled. Vell was a cool as nigga. I fuck with him, but I don't agree with the fuck shit he does.

"I'm trying to see why you thought it was a good idea to bring another female here and you knew Leah was going to be here? I know the two of you ain't together and the two of you are going through your bullshit but bringing another bitch in won't help at all. It gives her more of the reason to say fuck you." I argued. Leah was my granddaughter too. Her grandmother Harriet Jean was my best friend. Damn, I miss OG Harriet J. I've been looking after Leah for as long as I can remember and that'll never stop.

"I hear you OG Lou, but damn Leah isn't a saint. I almost killed her a few weeks ago. She's been keeping company with another man and I haven't acted on it. What the fuck am I supposed to do? I don't want to be out here entertaining different women but I'm tired of being by myself. I'm sorry, what more do I have to do?"

"Look Vell, Leah isn't your average female. I raised her. Does she love you? I know she does. Sometimes I'm sorry isn't enough. Your bag isn't enough. You hurt my baby and it's taking a little more time for her to bounce back. Flexing with another female, it'll never get you back in her good graces. Actions speak louder than words." I finished wrapping with Vell. He knew he was wrong if Leah did meet somebody, she's not rubbing it in his face to be messy. I'm not with that messy shit, period.

It was getting late. I made my way into the living room to check on my Christmas Tree to make sure it's coming together good. Hell, Malone would rush my shit to make sure her shit is better than mine. I noticed Leah was a little distant. I'm sick of her and Vell. I noticed she was trying to slip out. I walked up right behind her and grabbed her jacket.

"Come here Leah, what's up with you Ms. Lady? I'm always here for you if you need anything. Talk to your OG and tell me what's going on."

"I know OG Lou. I appreciate you. I'm just going through some things, but it's working itself out."

"What's up with you and Vell?" I asked I wanted the tea because last I heard he was still running up behind her, trying to get her to come back.

"Nothing, I met someone OG Lou and I'm happy. I like him and he's a grown ass man. I want you to meet him one day." She beamed. No wonder Leah wasn't tripping. She had someone else occupying her time.

"I would love that. Why didn't you bring him to eat with us?"

"Because I like him, and I don't want Vell ruining that for me. I fucked up and let him kill Cohen but with him, I refuse to risk it. I care about him, he's good people. I have a date. He made US a Thanksgiving dinner so I'm sneaking out to cuff with a boss." She beamed.

"Damn does he have an uncle or granddaddy with some pimpin' for your OG?"

"I'll see." I smacked hands with Leah and she ran up out of here. Vell better get his shit together because she'll be gone with whoever her secret is.

Chapter 9

Leah

Malone walked me to my car. I really wish she wouldn't have. The last thing I needed was for Sphinx and Vell to walk out here and fuck up my vibe. I have something special to look forward to when I leave here. I guess we could fire up a blunt and puff and pass it a few times before I leave. I didn't even want to come here because I knew that I would run into Vell. I've been having Thanksgiving at OG Lou's for as long as I can remember. I'm not even bothered that he's with somebody. I'm glad he has somebody. I just didn't need it to be in my face because I for damn sure wasn't in his.

OG Lou read his ass. I wanted to laugh so hard, but I kept it classy. Vell wanted me to entertain that bullshit, but I wasn't. I tried so hard to sneak out earlier but OG Lou was on my fuckin' heels. She snatched me up so quick, I couldn't do shit but laugh. I was trying to see my baby. I couldn't wait to see Malik.

I haven't seen him in a few weeks and I missed his ass something serious. I look forward to our conversations. I'm looking forward to our link up. Malone and I got in my car. Thank God I had the push to start. I cranked the heat up, making sure it was a little toasty. I grabbed the blunt out of my ash tray, fired it up, took two pulls and passed it to her. Damn, that felt good.

"Leah, what's going on, why are you leaving? You've been acting funny lately. I've been giving you, your space but I want to let you know that I'm not feeling this shit at all." She argued. Malone went straight in. I've been distant lately, but I have my reasons.

"I know Malone and I'm sorry. I've been going through some shit and I don't want to bother you with my problems. You know how I get when I'm in my zone. You're married now, so we can't sit on the phone and rap like we used to or even kick it like that. I can't call you to turn a few corners with me or even go to the club with me. Shit changed when you said I do. I'm happy for you because you deserve that. I got to deal with my shit on my own."

"Leah don't do that, please don't. Just because I'm married doesn't mean shit. If you call me, I'm fuckin' coming regardless of who I'm married too, and I still expect the same from you. Sphinx knows that I'm never too busy for you because you've always been there for me.

You're my best friend and my everything. I would never trade our bond for any man. You were there way before him and if he ever decides to leave, I know you'll still be here."

"I appreciate that. Real bitches do real shit and that's why you my bitch. You and I both know that nigga ain't going no damn where. I met someone, Malone. His name is Malik. I like him. We've been talking for a few weeks now." I beamed. I can't think of the last time I was excited about a nigga I met. It's been a minute.

"Bitch I heard about him. I didn't want to come right out and ask you about it. I knew you would tell me. Vell came to the house and he was pissed, he caught you with him or some shit? I was outside of Sphinx's man cave listening. Bitch you know I'm nosey. Spill the fuckin' tea."

"What did you hear? I'm not surprised. Malik and I went out on a date and as soon as it ended, he walked me to my door. He was holding me up against the base of my front door. My legs were wrapped around his waist. I wanted that nigga in the worst way. I didn't want him to let me go. As soon as I walked in Vell was sitting in my loft sitting on my couch looking all crazy. Malik is a grown ass man and a real fuckin' boss. He made cum without even touching me."

"Bitch, you can keep a fuckin' secret hoe. Gawd damn I knew it was something. I'm so happy for you. Bitch Vell crazier than a motherfucka. You deserve it. Are you really feeling him or it's just something to do? If he makes you smile the way you're smiling now, let him."

"No bitch I like him a whole lot. That's why I'm moving with caution because I don't want anything to happen to him. I got to head out of here because he made us a Thanksgiving dinner. I might give him some dessert if he plays his cards right."

"Oh shit, don't tell me nothing else, please don't. I can't even brag and fuck with Vell because he's my brother in law and I'm married to his brother. Damn you ain't playing fair. Don't put that pussy on him, if so, it's a wrap." She laughed.

"Malone you already know. IF I bless this nigga with a piece of me it's a wrap and guess what, a bitch ain't scared. Vell was the last nigga I fucked and that was six months ago. It's a new day. I'm ready to cock these legs open."

"DON'T DO IT, BITCH. Please don't." She begged.

"Fuck Vell, I'm not tripping off him. I want to Malone. It's something that I want to do. I've been saving myself for months. I've had opportunities to fuck plenty of niggas, but I didn't want too. My pussy has a few miles on it. The next nigga I fuck is going to be my husband, not just a random. It's deeper than sex. It could be in love because it doesn't feel like lust. He's different and I'm hooked on him. I got a crazy ass fetish for him. I'm addicted to his touch. I'm infatuated with his appearance. I can smell his cologne and he's not even near me. Bitch, he got me wide open. His conversation has me mesmerized." I admitted. I can't believe I said that shit. I bit my bottom lip.

"Oh my God Leah. I'm speechless. If he makes you feel like that don't let that shit go for anybody. It is what it is. I want to see you in love even if it's not with Vell. It's not your fault he cheated. You know I can't judge you. I can't wait to meet my new brother in law."

"Thank you. He wants me to fly out to Houston with him in a few weeks. He's the district manager at Top Golf. I think he does something else too. I know he does something else. The district manager is a cover up. I wish you could come with me."

"I wish I could too, but you know Sphinx ain't having that at all. I think you should go and go with the flow and see where all the roads lead too? We know it ain't Zone 6. Where's he from, please don't say our hood?" She asked.

"No bitch, I got me a real Hot Boy. Louisiana bred, born, and raised."

"Okay baby, I see you bitch." Malone and I slapped hands with each other.

"Bitch when that nigga calls me his Baby or his Juvie? I go insane. I'm telling you I'm fucking his ass tonight." I heard a knock at my window. Malone and I looked out the window and it was Layla.

"Y'all got me fucked up." She yelled. Malone hit the unlock and let Layla in.

"Damn y'all bitches out here getting blazed without me. Y'all keeping secrets and shit. What the fuck did I miss?" She argued and laughed. I love Layla to death but she's still Vell sister. I gave Layla the rundown on Malik.

"I'm happy for you. Even though I want you and Vell to work it out. Don't tell me shit else about him because I don't want to know about it. The less I know the better." She laughed.

"Layla honey, Leah's new boo is taking her to Houston. I'm feeling him, and I haven't even met him. Bitch don't tell Vell. She extended an invite but quickly took it back," she laughed. Malone ain't shit.

"Malone don't do me. I didn't tell Sphinx about you when you were pregnant with his babies in prison. I just don't want to know about it. If he asks me, he won't be able to tell if I'm lying or not and I don't want to be in the middle at all." I had to respect Layla's wishes.

"I feel you, Layla. Malone shut up, you're married. Sphinx isn't about to let you go out of town on a girl's trip? Girl bye! Layla, you can come with me. Shon and Malone can baby sit." We laughed at Malone. "Sphinx can smell you a mile away." We finished laughing and kicking it. Shit, I had to go because Malik was calling me.

"Ok Ladies I'll get up with you later. It's time to get Boo'd up with a boss." I had to leave OG Lou's quick. I didn't want Vell to follow me. I can't be living like this. I've been waiting on this day for weeks. I had my hoe bag packed. I wanted to see if he could stimulate my body as well as he stimulates my mind. I have never wanted to fuck a nigga as bad as I wanted to fuck him. Maybe it was because he was different.

It wasn't about the pussy for him, it was about me. We didn't meet off the strength of him getting the pussy and his bag was the only reason I was fucking with him. Malik called back. I had to answer the phone this time. I answered on the third ring.

"Hello." His voice blurred through my Bluetooth speakers. I loved the way he sounds.

"Hey Ms. Lady, how are you? I've been waiting for you for a few hours now. Dinner is ready and I'm waiting for you to eat." He explained. Damn, I could get used to this. He says all the right things.

"I'm on my way Malik, I'm headed your way now." I smiled. I was whipping it down Candler Road about to hop on I-20E to I-285S. I couldn't wait to make it to him.

"You better be. I'm waiting for you, Ms. Lady."

"I'm coming baby, you don't have to wait too much longer." I sassed. I was laying it on real thick. I could tell he was feeling it.

"Alright watch yourself with that baby, shit. You ain't ready for that." Shit if he only knew what the fuck, I was ready for.

"Whatever baby." I mocked him, as I cooed into the phone.

"Alright baby please bring your ass on." Malik and I hung up the phone with each other. He didn't have to tell me twice. I was on my way. I had the biggest smile on my face and it wasn't even because I was sneaking around with him. I wanted in him the worst fuckin' way. I pulled up to the address that Malik provided me. Damn, he had a nice ass home ducked off in Ellenwood, Georgia. I popped my trunk and grabbed my hoe bag.

I rang the doorbell. It took a minute for him to answer. I started toying with my phone because I knew he was fuckin' with me. He finally opened the door. He took my phone out of my hand and put in his pocket. He grabbed my bag out of my hand, then took my hand and led me into his home. It smells amazing in here.

"I'm glad you finally made it. I thought I was going to have to comb the streets looking for you." He explained. He knew I was coming.

"If I wasn't, I would've never answered the phone. I told you I was coming. Don't my word count for something?" I asked. I placed my hand on my hip and I tried so hard not to let him see me bite my bottom lip. He pulled me in for a hug. Malik was a low-key thug. I swear I loved being wrapped up in his arms. Damn, he smells so good. I can tell he would never bring me any harm.

"Aye Leah, your skin is so soft I can't wait to get lost in it." He slurred. Malik was tipsy. I could smell the liquor and weed on his breath.

"Oh yeah?" I asked. Let me be honest for a minute, he's the only hood nigga I've ever understood. I get him. He stands out above the rest. I placed my free hand on his chest. He cupped my chin and stole a kiss. Damn this nigga was romantic. What the fuck do I even know about this shit?

"Come on, let's eat." I sat my coat on Malik's ottoman. I had on my cute little black Gucci fitted dress. I could feel him staring a hole through me. I had chills running up my legs. I was scared to turn around. He was making me so fuckin' nervous. I felt him walk up behind me. My heart was beating so fast that I hope he couldn't hear it.

"Back up and give me some space please." I pouted. I could feel him breathing down my neck. Damn, he makes me nervous. I've had these panties on all day and I'm not trying to fuck them up before I sit down and eat.

"I haven't seen you in two weeks what the fuck do you expect? I thought you missed me?" He asked. He wrapped his arms around my waist and bit my neck. I wish he wouldn't have done that.

"I did miss you and I'm here now. I'm starving. I didn't even eat because I wanted to eat with you. My OG Lou out here looking at me like I'm crazy because I'm passing up meals and shit." I laughed.

"Good you should've told her your man cooked for you." He chuckled.

"My man? I told her I was eating dinner with a friend." I sassed. I tilted my head back on his shoulders. I gave him a menacing stare. I'm trying to see if he was for real or not.

"Oh, I'm still in the friend zone lil baby? I thought I was moving up? I guess I'll have to put in a little more work. Meet me halfway Leah that's all I'm asking. It takes two, you and me." He stated. He pointed at my heart and his.

"We're friends Malik but trying to get to know each other. I'm willing to meet you half way." I smiled. I'm willing to try. Malik looked at me as if he didn't believe me. I tried to shake it off and ignore it. I would love to be more than friends, but I can't right now. I'll have to move with caution. I don't like what hurt feels like. Malik had the table setup real nice. I went to the sink and washed my hands. I grabbed a plate and Malik snatched it out of my hands.

"Sit down Leah. Tell me what you want? I got this." He argued. He chastised me as if I were a kid.

"Excuse me, I want to try everything," I argued. "I can feed myself." Malik started fixing our plates. He had mine loaded with turkey, dressing, baked mac n cheese, mashed potatoes, green bean casserole, candied yams. Malik slid my plate in front of me. He took a seat right in front of me. He grabbed my hand and said grace.

"Lord, this meal is the work of your hands that you have provided for me, yet again, and I am forever grateful. I confess my tendency to forget to ask for your blessings upon my life, and Leah's life. Through the comforts that You have given me to enjoy. So many people lack these daily comforts and it is selfish of me to forget about them in their time of need. Show me how to make the most of your blessings in my life, for everything I have is a gift from you. In Jesus' Name, Amen."

"Amen." Malik and I started eating. The food was good. I was impressed. I caught him catching glances at me while I was eating. I wiped my mouth and stood up from the table. I was full already. I started putting the food away, then I ran the dish water, so I could wash the dishes. It's only right I help. That's the last thing I could do since he cooked all the food. I helped Malik clean the kitchen. He made a strawberry pie, but I couldn't eat anymore. He fed me a spoon full of it and it was good. I dried the counters off and wiped the table. I went to get my hoe bag and Malik jumped up immediately behind me.

"What's wrong Leah, where are you going?" He asked. I stopped in my tracks and turned around to face him to see what's up. I brought a bag with me, so I didn't plan on leaving until tomorrow.

"Nothing is wrong Malik. I'm good and I'm full. I just wanted to take a hot shower and change into my pajamas, is that cool?" I asked. "My feet are killing me."

"I'll massage them for you. Oh yeah, it's cool. You just got up and didn't say anything, so I didn't know. You got to let a nigga know something." He stated.

"I'm sorry, show me to the bathroom."

"First door on the right." I finally made my way to the bathroom, because I needed a hot shower. I wanted to get comfortable and lay up under Malik. I had some cute little lace boy shorts and a sports bra. I slid my pajamas out of my bag and laid it on the toilet. I grabbed all my toiletries and placed them on the sink. Coco Chanel Bodywash was my fragrance of choice. I cut the shower on and adjusted it to my liking. I stepped in the shower and it was steaming hot. I stepped in and started lathering my body. I had a lot of shit on my mind.

My mind was in a million places. The only place I wanted to be right now was here. I refused to sit at home alone and shed another tear. Malik was my only focus. I kept questioning myself about was I making the wrong decisions with Vell. I'm sick of it. I can't dwell on the what if's right now. I finished handled my hygiene because I was using all his hot water up and got out as quickly as possible. I didn't realize that I was in here this long the water started to turn cold. I cut the water off and pulled the shower curtain back. I reached to grab a towel and felt a pair of my hands brush up against mine. I jumped and covered myself up. It was Malik. I didn't want him to see me naked.

"I didn't mean to scare you. I was trying to make sure you were straight, you were in here for a long time."

"I tend to get lost in hot and steamy situations. Can you get out of here while I put my clothes on?" I asked. He just wanted to come in her while I was naked.

"Is that right? Why do you want me to get out? I've seen plenty of naked women before, but I like looking at a naked Leah," he chuckled and smirked.

"Yep. It's a difference between me and other women. Get out so I can put my clothes on please." I pouted and pulled the curtain back. Malik snatched the curtain back.

"I want to see you. I can help you put your clothes on Leah."

"I know, but I want to do it all by myself."

"Too bad because I want to help you. It's time I get acquainted with your body measurements." Malik grabbed my hand and led me out the shower. I stood in front of him. He grabbed my lotion off the sink, and he poured a handful in his hands. He grabbed my thighs and started applying lotion to both legs. I closed my eyes and said a quick prayer. I hope I don't come on myself fucking with him. He started rubbing the lotion on my calves. He was eye level with my pussy. He inhaled it. My juices were dying to bless his tongue. I wonder how wet his mouth could get? He sat me down on the toilet and started applying lotion to my feet.

"You have pretty feet." He stated.

"Thank you." I blushed and gave him a faint smile. He fucked me with his eyes lustfully. I watched him bite his bottom lip. He handed me my boy shorts. I took them out of his hands and he snatched them from me. Malik held my shorts out for me to step in them. He had a devilish grin on his face. He was up to something.

"Malik, why are you playing with me?" I pouted. I didn't have time for his shit.

"I'm just trying to see what you're working with? I'm trying to see if that big ass bounces when you're, lifting those big old legs? I want to see you squeeze into these little ass shorts. I want to see if that pussy squirt if I give you some head. I want to see them titties bounce when I got you face down." He slurred. Malik was feeling himself. I couldn't be alone with him. I for damn sure didn't want to put my shorts on because my pussy was wet as fuck. My juices were liable to run down my legs at any given moment. I don't like what he does to my body. I snatched my shorts out of his hands. I tried to put them on quickly. Malik stood behind me and finger fucked my pussy wet. He opened the flood gates. He ate my pussy from the back.

"Stop." I moaned. It wasn't supposed to happen like this at all.

"Why do you want me to stop Leah?" He asked. Why would he want to know the question to an answer he already knows? He knew what the fuck he was doing to my body.

"I just do." I moaned. Malik ignored me and continued to eat my pussy. I tried to break free from his embrace, but he wouldn't allow it.

"Can you please stop?" I pouted and moaned. He wasn't listening. The only sounds that could be heard throughout the room was him lapping up my juices. My body shook. I was trying to hold on to him for support. He removed my hands. I swear if I fall, I'm going off.

"Tell me why Leah? If you fall, I'll catch you." He slurred and moaned.

"I don't like the way my body responds to you. I don't like the way you make me feel." Malik raised up and wiped his mouth off. He sat me down on the toilet seat and stood in my face. I was trying to read him.

"Leah when I touch you, how does it feel? When I hold you, do you like it? Baby, be honest, keep it real with a nigga. I'm feeling the shit out of you, but I don't need you holding back. I got you. I'm asking you to trust me. I swear I want to take you down some roads you never been before. You got to meet me half way baby."

"I am. I'm open to doing that."

Malik finished putting lotion on me, then he helped me put on my boy shorts and sports bra. He toyed with my nipple rings. He was so fuckin' attentive to me it's crazy.

What the fuck is he trying to do to me? I'm not trying to fall in love no time soon. He gave me a big bear hug. I swear I didn't want to let him go. I wrapped my legs around his waist. He grabbed the elastic on my shorts and it popped my back. He gripped my ass cheeks.

"Ouch, Stop Malik." I moaned.

"You don't tell me what to do. Boys do what they can, and men do what they want." He argued. I wrapped my arms around his neck. He placed soft bite marks on my neck. He carried me to the sofa and laid me on his chest. His hands roamed my backside.

"Are you ready to be honest with me about what we're doing here?" He asked. He cupped my chin, making me look at him. Why is he doing this? I wasn't ready to reveal this.

"Let me keep it real with you Malik. I don't want to tell you how I feel. I rather keep it to myself. Somethings are better left unsaid. I'm trying to heal myself. I'm afraid of expressing myself. I may reveal too much." I sighed. That was the truth. I care about him and it's crazy.

"Damn Leah don't shut a nigga out. I want you to know how I feel about you. I want you to know what my intentions are. I always want you to be honest with me. If I have a real chance let a nigga know something. I don't want this to be for nothing. I want to get use to this. I love the time that we've spent together. I want to know when I'm fuckin' up. I want to know when I'm doing everything right because I don't want to lose sight. I want you to be the high light of my life." He explained. I've never been so open with anybody. I'm about to be open with Malik. I don't feel like I should back away. What the fuck do I have to lose? I hope I don't regret this shit.

"I'm addicted to your touch, and that's a bit much. I feel like it's too soon, but I can see my heart has a mind of her own and she's making room for you. I love being wrapped up in your arms. Promise me you won't cause me anymore harm? I have a few layers built up protecting my heart. I'm opened to letting you pull a few back. That's a start."

"Leah the heart wants what the heart wants. The sooner you stop fighting it the better you'll be. Listen to your heart and whenever you're ready to give it to me. I promise to take really good care of it." He revealed. He placed a wet kiss on my lips. He revealed. I believed him for some reason. My trust is so fucked up, but I feel like I could trust him. It's crazy, I'm willing to trust a stranger. I trusted Vell and he was living a fuckin' lie. I can't compare Malik and Vell to each other because they're both different. Life has a funny way of showing you some shit that you're not ready for.

"I hear you."

"I want you to listen to me. Trust the process, Leah. I'm not out to hurt you." He revealed. He placed a wet kiss on my lips. He started tugging at my hips.

"What are you trying to do to me, Malik?"

"I want to do a lot of things to you Leah, but Baby, you ain't ready for a nigga like me in your life. I'm willing to take it as slow as possible. The ball is in your court. Let me know when you're ready for that one on one? I want to coach US to the finish line in time."

"What makes you think I'm not ready?" I asked. I tried to raise up off him. He was determined to hold me in place. Malik was affectionate. I loved that about him. I swear he would be the perfect boyfriend. I hope this wasn't a front to get the pussy. I wanted to get a good look at him to see if I could read him.

"You're holding back, and I can't do shit but respect that. You're not ready Leah and that's okay. I like you enough to wait. I'm not giving you any space. I want to be in your corner. I respect you for being open and honest with me. We both got baggage. I've done my share of shit and I'm sure you have too. I'm on my grown man shit. I'm not with the games and shit. I can't change the past and I can't erase what that nigga did to you. I want to take care of your heart. I care about you. I know I don't want to be your friend to much longer. I know what I want."

"Why me? What separates you from the rest Malik? If I give you my heart who's to say you won't break it?" I asked.

"Why not you? I want you to be the one. I want to love you how you should be loved? I want to do more than cuff you. Actions speak louder than words. I'll keep showing you. I don't have a problem with that." Malik and I sat up and talked until we both fell asleep. I can't think of the last time I've slept this well. I was comfortable laying on top of him.

I wanted to fuck him so badly just to see what he was working with, but it'll only complicate things. I got to get my shit together. I don't want to lose Malik. He said he's willing to wait but how long? Shout outs to Vell for putting me in this situation.

I finally made it home. I enjoyed my night with Malik. It was different. I'm feeling how different he is. I didn't want to leave him, but he had to go to work. As soon as I threw my car in park. My door was snatched open and it was Vell. Damn, I just wanted to have my moment. My smile was quickly turned into a frown because I didn't want to see him. I politely closed my door and I tried to pull off. He opened my car door up and threw my car back in park. I'm moving. I'm sick of him popping up at my shit. He grabbed my shirt and pulled me out of the car.

"Why are you here Vell? You and I aren't together. That's been understood months ago. Quit popping up at my shit. Stop fuckin' grabbing on me. Damn Vell, I haven't popped up at your spot one time. I'm moving on. Why are you mad at me? I haven't done shit to you." I argued. I folded my hands across my chest. I'm sick of him

"Leah, you know why I'm fuckin' here? Where in the fuck did you sleep at last night, because you didn't sleep here?" He argued. He has everybody in my fuckin' business. Vell is out here making a scene and we're not together. I wish the fuck I would pull up at a niggas house asking questions that I already know the answer too.

"I don't know why you're here. Wherever I lay my head is my business, it ain't yours. The same bitch you brought to OG Lou's house, go run up on her to see where she laid her head at. Better yet get that bitch a bird's nest." I laughed. Vell didn't like that shit at all. He stepped all in my personal space.

"Aye, you better stop fuckin' playing with me. I ain't tripping off no duck ass bitch, period. On some real shit Leah, I'm not with all this sucker free shit. I hope you ain't out here giving this nigga hope? If you fucked him last night, I'm killing him tonight. I got eyes on you even when you think you're sneaking around on me, you ain't. It took everything in me not to run up in that nigga shit and murk his ass and you. My OG saved you. You better count your blessings. She called me last night while I was sitting in front of his crib. My mask was on and I wasn't about to use a silencer. She asked where I was at because she was in town to see us. I don't know why I told her the truth, but that shit rolled off my tongue. She told me to come see her and not to take old boy's life. I listened to her and I didn't realize that I fucked up until I pulled off. After I left my OG's house. I rode back through there and your car was still parked, and the hood was cold. I knew you weren't leaving. I knew you were fuckin' this nigga. My OG called me again to see if I made it home yet and I lied because I wanted to handle my business. You're my fuckin' business. As soon I stepped out the car about to sneak up in that motherfucka. She tapped me on my shoulders and told me to take it home. Tread fuckin' lightly Leah, because you're reaching. Next time I'll cut my phone off and nobody will be able to stop me." He argued and threatened.

"Why do you want to deny me of my happiness Vell? I played shit cool when you were with your date last night. I respected you and I could've shown out, but for what? You're not my man. You cheated on me. I'm facing my reality we're not together. Keep flaunting those bitches in my face. I hope they make you happy. I don't even want to flaunt him in your face because you won't even respect what the fuck I got going on, but you will soon if this nigga continues to play his cards right. I'm not on any get back shit. Any nigga that I'm out in the open with its official and he has a lot of potential." I argued. I don't give a fuck about hurting his feelings because he didn't give two fucks about mine.

Why couldn't break ups be simple? Vell and I have been going through the same shit for months and I'm sick of it. Maybe it's not meant for us and I'm okay with that. I don't think I could take him back, because he would always be that nigga that fucked a bitch that smiled in my face. Mignon wasn't my friend, but an associate. Oh, but Vell was my man and my fiancé. It'll always be in the back of mind. I can't trust a motherfucka like that. I just can't.

"Leah, do you think it's about to go down like that? You can kill all that shit. Why can't I come back home? Why can't we work it out? I changed Leah just because you see me with a bitch that don't mean shit. Every bitch out here knows you're my wife. My home is always with you. I want to come back home. Tell me what I got to do? I'm trying Leah, meet a nigga half way." He argued.

"It's not going down how you want it too. I want you to leave me alone Vell. I'm trying to change too. Just without you. Give me my space. I didn't ask for space, you gave me this shit voluntarily for free nigga. My OG didn't raise no fool Vell. I don't give a fuck what these bitches know. I've heard that before. A bitch can know their place all day, but your words mean nothing to me because you didn't hold your end up.

Guess what these niggas know? I'm up for grabs but the next nigga I fuck and give my heart to will be my husband. Guess what Vell, this nigga is in the running." I argued. I grabbed my purse out of my seat and I tried to walk off. Vell grabbed me and wrapped his arms around me.

"It ain't no breaking up."

Chapter 10

Layla

I've been back in Atlanta for about nine months now. It's cool being back home. I had to shop for some new winter clothes, thigh high boots, short skirts, and shit. Oops, I forgot I was with Shon this season. I'm taking a trip to New York for fashion week. I loved living in Miami. I loved wearing no fuckin' clothes. I miss my city so much. I'm going back for Haitian Day. I miss the beaches and bottles. I miss cruising the city and I miss posting up on South Beach. I miss hopping on a cruise ship whenever the fuck I wanted too, just to escape the bull shit. I miss going to the hood to get me some bomb ass soul food. I miss every fuckin' thing.

I miss Trecie and Tati. Don't get me wrong, Malone and Leah are cool but ain't no bitches like the ones I got. Even though they dropped the dime on me with Shon's ass. I wouldn't trade them for anything in this world. I missed home too and being able to see my brothers whenever I wanted too. Shon is a wonderful father. Shalani loves him and she looks exactly like him. I thought things would be different by now. Shon made a lot of promises when he forced me to move back to Atlanta. The only thing that he came through on is being a wonderful father. Call me crazy, but the moment I stepped off that plane, and he slid that ring back on my finger. I knew we would've been married by now.

I try so hard not to complain and dwell on that shit, but it fucks with me mentally and physically. I try so hard not to bother my mother or Leilani with this shit and keep things to myself. I swear some days I just want to pack my shit up and leave his ass again because I'm tired of playing with Shon. I'm too grown for the games and shit. I'm not these bitches he used to fuckin' with. He knows exactly who the fuck I am. I don't need his money in case he forgot. I run the Baptiste Cartel. I sign off on every fuckin' thing. Sphinx and Vell ain't selling shit unless I sign off on it. I know something better change soon or else I'll be gone in the wind. My phone started ringing and it was my mother. I answered on the first ring.

"Hey mommy, how are you? I miss you." I beamed. I love my mother so much. I wish she was here instead of Haiti, but she deserves to be happy and who am I to deny her of that, especially after the bull shit my father pulled.

"I'm sure you do. Where's my little princess? It's a new sheriff in town." She asked. My mother had Shalani spoiled. Every other week we were getting packages in the mail from her.

"She's asleep." I sighed. Shalani's sleeping habits were pretty good. I couldn't complain. I couldn't allow her to sleep long because she would be up all night.

"What's wrong with you Layla? You've had the baby, what's the problem now? Go out and let your hair down. Malone will baby sit or Leilani," she stated. My mother knew me better than I knew myself. She knew something was bothering me.

"Mommy it's not that simple. I swore I would never be one of those mothers who dropped their child off to party and bull shit. I'm just tired. I don't want to go out." I explained. Going out to a club wouldn't solve any problems. Shon stepping the fuck up would.

"Talk to me Layla, I'm here. What's going on?" She asked. I had to tell her what's up or else she would keep pressing for the information. I had to be honest with her.

"Mommy, when I was away from Shon all of those years. I had so much fuckin' confidence. I demanded attention and my fuckin' respect. Cree and I were together for three years and we were engaged and planning a wedding. He knew what he wanted. He knew I wouldn't tolerate his shit. All he had was three years tops and if we didn't know what we were doing by then I was moving on.

I've been with Shon for a long ass time and I don't care how long we were apart. Time isn't on his side. If we're not getting married, then I'm not sitting around. I'm not fuckin' doing it. We can co-parent. Do you think I'm selfish? We know each other already. What else do I fuckin' need to know? I didn't pursue him, he pursued and trapped me."

"Layla Renee watch your fuckin' mouth. You can't compare Shon to Cree. There's no comparison. I know you loved Cree, but he was keeping secrets. I can't say that he wasn't genuine. I know he loved you, but he knew your father was alive. I know you're upset.

I know you love Shon, but don't fuckin' settle. I don't give a fuck who it is. It's only one Layla Renee Baptiste in this world and I gave birth to her. It's not a female walking that's weighing up to you. You have a lot to offer any man. If he's not doing what you want him to do, then leave. Don't think twice about it. You're a grown ass woman Layla. I've schooled you enough. At this point in your life, you don't need my guidance. If this situation is heavy on your mind, you and Shalani can come here. Don't back track with him. Shon better step the fuck up or he'll miss the boat. AGAIN. I'm rooting for him, but if he doesn't make it than oh well.

I feel where you're coming from. Don't lose yourself baby girl. You've come a long way. Your daughter is a blessing. You wanted a child. You wanted to have sex with him. He gave you something to remember him by. I don't care how much you love him, don't be anybody's fool. Do you want to marry him, Layla? Are you still in love with him?" She asked. My mother just gave me the business in a matter of minutes. I know what I need to do and I'm going to leave because I keep thinking about it.

"I love Shon and of course I want to marry him. I feel like I'm settling momma and I refuse to settle. I'm leaving. I got to. I keep thinking about it and my mind is made up. I'm not going to pressure Shon any more or ask him to do anything that he doesn't want to do."

"Do what's best for you Layla. I support you. If you leave this time, let him know your whereabouts. A child is involved and don't keep Shalani away from him just because you and Shon are going through your little issues. I know Shon, he doesn't want to lose you or his daughter to another man. Apply pressure on his ass. Stand for something and never fall for anything." She explained. My mother and I finished talking for another thirty minutes. I enjoyed our conversation. I needed to have this talk with her. Shon better get his shit together because I'm tired of sitting around waiting on shit to change. I'll fuck around and change the forecast on his ass. Haiti or Miami, shit maybe even California. I know Chenae is ready to pick me up from the airport.

Vell

Me and Sphinx where handling some business. My phone kept going off. I forgot to cut my phone off. I never have my phone on when I'm making plays. I know it wasn't my OG or Layla because they knew what time we were at the warehouse distributing our product. We had a big ass shipment come in from Haiti. The ports were hot in Savannah, so we had to reroute that shit. We've been here since 9:00 a.m. breaking these packs down and we just finished the last two. As soon as Sphinx and I walked out my phone rang again, and it was ZO. I'd call him back as soon as I get closer to the city. We didn't fuck around to tuff with these pigs out here in Augusta. I checked my call log and he's called me at least ten times. It must be an emergency. I threw Sphinx my keys and told that nigga to "DRIVE." He didn't ask any questions. He did as he was told. I hit ZO back asap and he answered on the first ring.

"Aye nigga is everything good?" I yelled. I don't know where Zo was at, but his background was loud as fuck. I hope that nigga isn't up to his old ways. Sphinx had Kevin Gates blasting in the background. He knew I was trying to make this call quick. I knew he was trying to get home to Malone. Thank God we didn't have a pack on us. He was doing 100 mph riding down I-20W.

"Hell no, shit isn't okay. You know Alexis and I flew out to Houston Tuesday for her cousin's funeral. Man guess who's staying at our Hotel?" He argued. I knew shit had to be serious.

"Sphinx turn the music down for a minute. Who was there Zo?" I wanted to know because I didn't know anybody out in Houston. I had a bad feeling about this conversation. I didn't have any enemies living.

"Leah and that motherfuckin' nigga I told you about at Top Golf a few weeks ago. OG Vell they're out here on some Boo'd up shit. I lit fire into Alexis and she swore she didn't know Leah was out here on some good bull shit. I knew she was lying. The only reason I didn't cut the fuck up was that our son was with us. Leah was scared as fuck, she already knew I was calling you. She knows I don't play that shit. You're my nigga, what you want me to do?

You coming out here to handle yours or do you want me to handle it? I can't give that nigga a pass twice. I know some niggas who know some niggas. I can make some shit happen." He argued. I swear Alonzo is always in the right place at the right fuckin' time. Leah was sneaky as fuck. She really thinks she's about to be with this nigga? I already warned her that's all she fuckin' gets. She really thinks we're done, never that.

"Oh yeah. It's going down like that? I can't give Leah or that nigga a pass. Send me the address to your hotel. I'll be there in a few hours and don't tell Alexis shit. Round them niggas up to see if they want to make some cash. I am coming for that ass. Aye, and call OG Roy and tell him to meet me in the hood." I argued.

"Bet, say less and bring your ass." I finished chopping it up with Zo. Leah really wants me to catch this niggas body, like I fuckin' won't.

"Aye Sphinx. I'm flying out to Houston tonight. Leah's on some real unfaithful shit. We're together regardless of what's going on in her thick skull. I need you to come with me, this shit ain't up for debate. Let me call our pilot to see if he can make a quick trip to Houston. Zo is already out there. I'm catching two fuckin bodies. Leah's and that niggas. She's hard headed as fuck. She wants that nigga dead. I ain't with that sucka free shit dog. I don't give two fucks about killing a nigga. I was born to kill." I argued. Leah had me so fuckin' hot. I can't wait to murk this nigga. Everybody knew Leah belonged to me. I guess this nigga didn't get the memo. I told Leah to get her black dress ready.

"Come on, why the fuck did you tell Zo to tell OG Roy to meet you in the hood. He's one nigga you don't want to call unless you fuckin' need him. Damn Vell. What the fuck am I supposed to tell Malone? Tonight's our date night. Are you sure you want to go out there and lay shit down?" He argued. Date night? Malone got my brother doing some corny ass shit.

"Tell Malone the fuckin' truth. Do you want me to tell her Leah got me fucked up? Shit, Malone can come too, because Leah will need her to carry her after I'm done. I swear I'm dragging that pussy ass nigga and Leah. I should've killed that nigga on Thanksgiving."

"I'm not telling her that Vell. What the fuck you mean you should've killed that nigga on Thanksgiving?

What the fuck did I miss?" He asked. I gave Sphinx the rundown of what happened. He just shook his head.

"I told Leah she better Thank God my OG was following me. I put that shit on the nigga nut sack that I came from. I would've murdered that nigga right in front of her and she would've been lying right beside that nigga in a pool of his blood. Sphinx, I'm a crazy ass nigga and you know that. She saw what the fuck I did to that pussy ass nigga when he pulled up at Leilani's. I ain't having that shit. She wants that nigga dead Sphinx, and guess what? I'll have his fuckin' head. She wants me to kill his ass."

"OG Vell you're hell. I'm riding with you right or wrong. Let's do this shit my way. If you gone kill this nigga, we gone kill 'em and head straight back home. I'm not fuckin' off in Texas with you and ZO. We'll have to make this shit as clean as possible. Shit is different in Texas. We'll be a long way from home. Let me call Lala to see if she can call Queen Helene to help us execute this shit the right way. We need a driver and a spot to dump this niggas body. She said she's our rider and she's riding right or wrong. We're going to find out.

I can't be away from home that long. My wife ain't having that shit at all. I ain't having that. I love lying next to Malone every night."

"I ain't trying to fuck off in Texas either. Let me call Lala to see if she still loves a nigga. She was mad at me about how that Leah shit played out. I know Helene gone ride with us. It's always fuck those other niggas when it comes to us. She's our OG. She goes hard in the paint and don't give two fucks about going to war with us."

"For sure, I already know that. Vell, I never got the chance to ask you, why did you do that shit? I told you when you and Leah got serious to cut Mignon off because that bitch didn't mean you any good. You didn't listen. You were too busy getting your dick wet and that bitch was for everybody. I knew she was going to get you in trouble. Bitches like Mignon, they want the bag regardless and they don't give a fuck who toes they step on to get it. She was wrong for still smiling up in Leah's face. You should've killed that bitch too."

"Look Sphinx, I know what the fuck I did was wrong and I'm paying for that shit every day. I don't need you reminding me. It's funny how the tables have turned because you were once in my shoes ruining my fuckin' engagement party. I'm not a dumb ass nigga. I kept fuckin' with Mignon because she was threatening to tell Leah.

I knew she wouldn't because she knows I'm a killer. Trust me, Yona can count her last fuckin' days because I'm hunting that bitch. I can guarantee you she won't live to see Christmas, fuck you mean. The moment my shit was aired out, all bets were off. It took me losing Leah to realize what the fuck I did was wrong. She didn't deserve that shit. I ain't never been a cheating ass nigga, that was you. I ain't never committed to no bitch out here but Leah. She got my heart and she can keep that shit, as long we can get back to what we used to be."

"I feel you because the thought of losing Malone had me going crazy. Momma raised us in the church, but we stayed away from that shit. She taught us how to pray and do all the right shit. The straight and narrow path wasn't the way for us. I know God probably isn't one of my biggest fans because I live a life of sin. I can't change that. I can try, but it's too late.

A lot of niggas pray for wealth and materialistic shit. I don't want God to give me anything that I don't need. When it's my time, it's my time and I'm gone shine regardless. We were raised to go out and get it out the mud or take that shit if necessary. A motherfucka ain't never gave us shit. We're takers by nature. I sat down and had a talk with God about me and Malone. When she got cased up and didn't fold on me despite all the lil shit we went through. I knew I had to get my shit together.

She could've said fuck me and told on me because she was innocent, and I was guilty. We didn't have any ties with each other besides the babies of mine that she was carrying that I didn't know about. I prayed for Malone to come back to me. I knew she was meant for me. I fucked up a few times but the thought of losing her made a nigga want to get it right. I ain't telling you what to do, but when you get Leah back don't take her for granted." He explained. I swear my brother done grew up on a nigga.

"I hear your ass nigga. I know Malone changed you and I ain't even mad at that shit. I knew shit was real at the bachelor's party. You were curving bitches left and right. In all my years of living, I thought I would never see the day my lil brother would curve bitches and pussy." I chuckled.

"Fuck you pussy ass nigga. For the right one, you'll curve every bitch. For Malone, I'll kill any bitch or nigga. You're curving bitches now and Leah hasn't even taken your pussy ass back. A bitch can't even smell or touch my dick." He argued and chuckled. Man, Malone put voodoo on my brother. Sphinx's married. I know the world is coming to an end, but that's a good look for him. "Slow this shit down nigga, you ain't driving a fuckin' four cylinder. This is a got damn V-12. I know you trying to make it home to wifey. I'm trying to make it to Houston to see my wife." Sphinx looked at me and start laughing and pressed the gas again. I know the dash board was reading at least 120 mph.

Chapter-11

Malone

I've been calling Sphinx for the past few hours and he hasn't answered the phone. He never does that. I blew up his phone just for the hell of it. I know he's been busy with work because of the Baptiste Cartel. Business has been extremely heavy since they took control. I don't give a fuck, he can still pick up the phone to call me. I worry about him whenever he leaves the house to handle his business. I pray he makes it back home to us. I hope everything is okay. He should've been home by now. I wanted to pull up at the Funeral Home and the Trap to see what's up.

It's just me here with the kids. My Auntie Linda Faye, she went to Haiti with my mother for the weekend. Let me find out she has a new boo too. I put the twins to sleep, Samaya and Kennedy were watching a movie, and Jah and Latwoin were playing the Play Station 4. Laylin and Lateef's sleeping habits are ridiculous. One day they'll sleep through the night and the next day they're up all night, and I let Sphinx deal with them.

I guess they knew their father wasn't home, so they decided to go to bed early. I had to do something to take my mind off Sphinx. Thank God I had my Kindle charged. I ran me a hot bubble bath. **Nique Luarks** dropped a hot new book that I've been dying to finish **You Set My Soul on Fire**. The tub was steaming hot to my liking and I poured myself a glass of wine.

I rolled a nice long blunt. I dipped my feet inside and wiggled my toes in the water. I stripped naked as soon as the water touched my body. I could feel the relaxation coming over me. I needed this bad. The only thing missing was Sphinx. I needed him. Tonight, was our date night. Every Saturday we had date night which consisted of a hot bubble bath and the two of us cuddled up in the tub. We didn't have a lot of alone time, but when we did, we made the best of it.

I missed my husband. I wanted to read him a few pages of this book. Sphinx loves to listen to me read these urban novels. The water finally had a nice hot warm chill to it. It felt so good. I had to relax and close my eyes for a few minutes.

I had a lot to be thankful for. It's been a minute since I've had a nice long talk with God. Our lives have changed a lot in a matter of a few months.

I'm married, and I have two new editions to my family. I gained another daughter who I love and adore as if she was my own. I gained three sons too. I'm blessed because I was in a fucked-up relationship for years up until a few months ago. I'm blessed and thankful to be in a different space. I heard the bathroom door open. I knew it was him. I smelled his cologne. It invaded my nostrils. I kept my eyes closed. I refuse to open them to acknowledge him.

"Baby, you started without me?" He asked. I wanted to bust out laughing. What the fuck did he think? He saw I was already in the tub relaxing and sipping without him. The only thing I haven't done was fire up this blunt. It's after 8:00 p.m. he should've been home. It's daylight savings and the street lights came on before he made it in. I don't play that shit.

I wasn't even about to respond because he knew I was mad at him. I heard his belt buckle touch the bathroom floor. He started undressing and getting in the tub. I watched him out the corner of my eye. He was watching me too. He lifted me up and sat me on his lap. He had a tight grip on my breasts. He slammed his dick inside of me and started hitting me with death strokes. I couldn't open my eyes if I wanted too. He started biting my neck. A few soft moans escaped my lips.

"Malone, I know you hear me talking to you? What the fuck did I do wrong that it has you giving me the cold shoulder?" He asked and grunted. I wanted the dick, that's all he's good for right now. He took a sip of my wine. I wasn't mad, he should've answered his phone when I called to let me know he's okay.

"I hear you Sphinx, but I'm not listening. I called you a few times because I wanted to talk and see how your day was going, but you didn't answer." I argued and moaned. I swear he doesn't want to go there with me. My attitude wasn't even supposed to slip out, that's what happens when you want to talk during sex.

"I got caught up Malone, and it's no excuse for me not answer my phone. I've been trying to figure out a way to tell you I got to catch a flight out to Houston in two hours. You know I was coming home to you for our date night. I wouldn't miss this for anything in this world. I missed you baby." He explained. I know he didn't fuck me senseless and drop a bomb on me. I raised up immediately to face him. I wanted to see what the fuck he means he was going to Houston? He held me down and continued to pound my pussy, so I wouldn't be able to raise up.

"Stop for a minute Sphinx." I moaned.

"Nope sit-down Malone and listen to me." He argued. Why is he raising his voice? He knew he said the wrong shit. He knew I would never agree to the bullshit he was spitting.

"Why can't I stand up and listen to you Sphinx? I need to look you in your face to see what type of lie you think you're about to run by me? Try me. What justifies you flying out to Houston without me? We don't have any family out there." I argued. I removed his hands. I looked him dead in his face. He gave me a menacing stare. I stared his ass back down. I wasn't budging. "You're not going period. You got me so fucked up."

"Malone, you know why I'm going to Houston. Your girl out there on some good bullshit. I got to ride with My OG to handle this business and I'm coming right back home, baby." He explained. Vell should've never cheated and we wouldn't be going through all this extra shit.

"Oh, so this is about Leah? We don't have shit to do with that. I swear Vell needs to give it up and let Leah live.

No, you're not going to Houston with Vell to go kill somebody. You heard what the fuck I said. Let Leah be, she's good and they're not together. Vell can speak with Leah when she comes back." I argued. "I swear I don't get these Baptiste men, y'all fuck up but don't want us to move on. Three words STOP FUCKIN' UP and you wouldn't have to catch bodies and chase women across the country." I argued.

"What the fuck are you trying to say? You weren't going anywhere period. I hear you Malone and I don't want to go. Do you think I want to leave my wife and kids to go out and do some hot ass shit? That's my brother, my OG. He raised me. We ride together and if it happens, we may die together. If he leaves this world before I do. I'll carry him, and he'll carry me. Please don't fight me on this shit. I tried to talk him out of it, but he's not trying to hear me out. I can't let him go out there alone." He argued. Tears poured down my face. I wiped my face with the back of my hands. I tried to raise up out the tub. He was really pissing me off.

"I said what the fuck I had to say. Don't fuckin go. Why does Vell want to go out there so bad? If they love each other than love will lead them back to each other." I argued. I wanted to see what the fuck does he mean he was going to Houston after I said no? He held me down, so I wouldn't be able to raise up. "Get off me."

"Sit down MALONE and listen to me. Men do things different then women. We love hard and we won't let anybody come in between something we love. Niggas fuck up sometimes. I'm not a saint nor do I want to be. Malone, for you I'll be a perfect ass nigga. Vell just wants to right his wrong. He's sorry. He gets it. I'm not vouching for him just because he's my OG.

We don't believe in letting love lead us back. We force our love back and apply pressure. We take chances, we put grips on hearts and hold them to make sure a nigga never steps in the way. If by chance he does, we'll put that nigga to rest. It is what it is, but that's how we're giving it up." He begged and pleaded.

"I've heard enough. Sphinx tell him not to go. If you cared about me and your kids, you wouldn't go." I cried. I pushed him. I wanted him to get the fuck away from me.

"Malone don't do that, because you know I love you and my children. What the fuck am I supposed to do? Malone meet me half way. Stop crying. I'm not trying to be the cause of your tears because no matter what I'm going to make it back home to you. My only agenda is to make sure my brother is straight and making it back home to my wife and kids." He argued. He doesn't get it, anything can happen to him.

"Sphinx and if he ain't straight?" I cried.

"It ain't no ain't. A motherfucka can't touch my brother without any repercussions. I can guarantee you it ain't going down like that. If it does Malone, I'm taking every motherfucka that was involved out. They'll see Vell when they reach hell. I put that shit on you baby." He argued.

"Good-bye Sphinx, because I don't know why we're even having this conversation. No matter what I say or how I feel your mind is already made up. You can leave now, you don't have to wait for two hours. Get to fuckin' stepping." I argued and cried. Sphinx killed my vibe. I tried to raise up out of the tub. He backed me in the corner and wrapped his arms around me.

"Move, let me go." I cried.

"No, I'm not letting you go, and you know that. Baby, please stop crying. I swear I'm not trying to upset you. Your opinion does matter. You fuckin' matter. I can't leave our home without us being on good terms. Malone, this ain't even us. This isn't how we rock. If something happened to Vell and I wasn't there to at least stand in the paint with him. My life would be fucked up because I would blame myself for his death.

My OG would blame me because I would never send my brother on a dummy mission on some territory that doesn't belong to us. I know ZO got Vell but that's my flesh. I got him I don't need another nigga to carry him. I can carry him on my own. I can't win for losing. I'll stay at home to pacify you and your feelings but if something happens to my brother. I won't forgive you because I could've been there. I mean that shit."

"What If something happens to you? What the fuck am I supposed to do? Don't make this shit about me. You're worried about if something happens to Vell. Sphinx, I'm crying because of YOU. Why does Vell want to go out there so bad? Damn, she's coming back home. Just go, Sphinx, I don't agree with it, but if something happens to Vell I don't want that on me at all. Go ahead and handle your business since you put it like that." I argued and cried. He cupped my chin forcing me to look at him. This conversation was over, and I didn't want to discuss it anymore. I hate that these tears are still pouring down my face fuckin' up my lashes.

"I'm not going, Malone. If I don't have your blessing. Motherfuckas will just deal with the consequences later. If something happens to my brother just know I won't be home until I kill every motherfucka involved." He argued.

"You do have my blessing to go Sphinx. When I married you, I accepted everything that came with you. I don't want you in the streets but you're still in them. Vell is a grown ass man and he knows right from wrong. It's not fair to me that he's dragging my husband out in the middle of the night because he fucked up his home.

I support you Sphinx, but this is the FIRST and LAST fuckin' time. Vell ain't got shit to lose because he doesn't have a wife or children, but YOU MY NIGGA you GOT A LOT TO LOSE. Get the fuck up out of my face. Go handle your business and make sure you make it back home." I argued. I tried to walk away from Sphinx. He grabbed me from behind and held me. His tongue traced the side of my neck. I hated he always did this whenever we had an argument.

"Malone, I love you and I appreciate you more than you will ever know. I'll never take you for granted. You run shit. Your word is law. Never question that. If I didn't have your blessing I wasn't going. I was willing to just let the cards fall where they lay."

"I love you too."

"I want you to love me, Malone? Promise me you'll never stop? Your love keeps me sane. Your love keeps me fed. I don't ever want to question when I'm lying in our bed does my wife love me or not. Your attitude had a nigga hot. I love how you put me on the spot. Never question what we got Malone."

"I love you Lateef. Why would you think I didn't? I only want what's best for you. When do we ever go all day without talking or checking in with each other? You switched up on us. Since we've been married it's been all about you and our family. Of course, I was going to express how I feel. I want to check Vell tonight but I'm not. As soon as you make it back home it's on. Hurry up and get out of my face before I change my mind."

"Why are you trying to rush a nigga off? I'm trying to make love to my wife before I catch this flight."

"The sooner you leave, the better because once that clock starts ticking it's wrap. I want you back home in 36 hours. We can make love when you come back."

"I want to make love now. Baby when I come back, I'm beating the pussy up because I missed it." I couldn't wait until Sphinx left so, I can shoot a text to Leah and let her know she has company in Houston. How did he even know?

MALONE - BEST FRIEND BECAREFUL YOU GOT COMPANY IN HOUSTON IN ABOUT 2 HOURS. JUST COME BACK HOME SO NOBODY GETS KILLED. PLEASE.

LEAH - COMPANY? ARE YOU SERIOUS?

MALONE - DEAD ASS BITCH. I WISH I WAS LYING. I HAD TO WARN YOU

LEAH - GOOD LOOKING OUT. ALONZO AIN'T SHIT. WE RAN INTO HIM AND ALEXIS. I HAD NO CLUE THEY WERE HERE OR STAYING IN THE SAME HOTEL. FUCK MY LIFE.

Chapter-12

Leah

I can't win for losing. Why me? I'm happy and I'm loving my happiness. I didn't know it was a crime for me to be happy. I couldn't even sleep last night because Vell consumed my thoughts. I wish he would just leave me alone like I asked him too. I swear if he shows up here on some bull shit I'm going off. Let me be, please. If I would've known it would've been this hard to get rid of Vell, I would've never gone out with his ass. That's what I fucking get for always bagging a street nigga. I just had to have his hoe ass, good dick bastard.

I knew Sphinx was crazy, but VELL was always low key and the older mature one. He's just as bad and to think I was laughing at Malone. The only thing I can do at this point is to pray. I like Malik, how can I not. He has me doing shit that I've never done. I don't want anything to happen to him because of me. It would hurt my soul if Vell does something to him. Why do I have to sacrifice my happiness because of him? It's not fair at all. I would never do Vell how he's doing me. I've been smiling the whole time I've been with Malik. I know Vell is up to no good. I can feel it. I'm not Malone I won't let Vell kill Malik. I'll walk away first.

"Baby, what's wrong? You've been acting distant all morning. Talk to me and tell me what's on your mind?" He asked. Malik walked up behind me and wrapped his arms around my waist line. He placed a few kisses on my neck. His touch sent chills through my body. My nipples were erect, and my pussy was tingling. I couldn't lie to Malik, he deserved more than that from me. Since I've met him, he's been nothing but good to me. I had to tell him the truth. I wouldn't want him out here walking around blind and not aware of his surroundings. I care about him.

"Malik, it's a lot wrong. You remember when we ran into Alexis and ZO yesterday? Zo and my EX are partners in crime. He ran his mouth and told my EX we were out here and he's on the way." I explained. Malik was looking at me very intense. He ran his hand across his waves. I know he was pissed. I had to tell him. I didn't want him looking at me sideways.

"Leah, I care about you a lot. I'm feeling you baby and I'm taking things as slow as possible with you. I'm going to ask you a question. I want you to answer it the best way you know how, but I want you to be honest with me. Do we have hope or does that nigga still have a chance?" He asked. Malik got straight to the point, of course, he has hope. I love the shit that we have going on. Vell wouldn't let us be great. I would be with Malik and run off in the sunset with him on some real shit. I would. I'm ready but I haven't said anything to him about it yet.

"Of course, you have a chance. If you didn't, I wouldn't be here. I wouldn't be doing any of this shit. I care about you Malik and I don't want anything to happen to you because of me." I explained. Malik pulled me into his arms and held me. He bit my bottom lip.

"Leah I ain't worried about him. May the best man win. It is what it is. I can hold my own if he wants to go there than we can. I ain't never backing down. He better ask about me. I ain't stepping on his toes and I refuse to let a nigga step on mine. I'm from the nine and we don't give two fucks about dying. We all got to go some day. I'll protect you with my life baby.

I haven't even sampled the pussy yet. I tasted it though and it was good as fuck. Peaches and cream. Sweet like I like it. I tongue fucked the shit out you. You came on my tongue a few times. I told you if you fall, I'll catch you. I want you to get up here and ride my tongue again. Baby, you got that dead man's pussy. I want to bless you with this dick so bad, but you ain't ready for me to take you down through there? A man knows when he's fucked up. Your EX fucked up and that's his fault. I can't wait to make you mine. I ain't gone never fuck up. I'm territorial as fuck, just wait until I try my luck." He explained. I swear I want to give him some pussy so bad. I know he'll take advantage of me. I can't wait to fuck the shit out of him.

"Malik try your luck. I'm begging you too." I pouted. I want him so fuckin' bad. I ain't never met a nigga that'll make me wait to get the dick. Malik was the first. How do I even know if he can fuck good if we haven't experimented with each other?

"Leah, I ain't trying to fuck you. I want to make love to you. You're not the type of woman I want to fuck. If so, I would've done that already. If I get the pussy now, I swear to God I'll kill that nigga. Don't let this district manager shit fool you, baby. Houston is my city. A nigga doesn't want to step on my toes. I guarantee you he'll wish he kept that pussy ass shit in the A. We play for keeps out here." He explained. I knew he was a goon.

"It's nothing wrong with us having sex Leah. It's not all about the pussy with me. I'm not looking for a fuck buddy. I told you that I'm a grown ass man. I can fuck a lot of women, but I only want to make love to one. I want something real. I didn't pursue you because I was after the pussy. I pursued you because I wanted to get to know you. I was captivated by your beauty. Once I got to know you, I wanted your heart baby. Sex complicates things, your EX he's acting a fool behind that pussy. I want to be a fool behind the pussy too, but not if we're not official." He explained.

"I'm speechless. I don't know what to say." I stated.

"Just trust the process and respect what I'm trying to do. You'll thank me later. Come on and let's get dressed. I got some places I want to show you. I got some roads I want to lead you too. Follow my lead, Leah." In a fucked-up world for some odd reason, I trusted him. I'm curious as fuck about him. I want him. I feel like I need him. In all my years of living, the only thing I ever needed from a man was some hard dick, a few fits, and wads full of cash, that's it. It wasn't even about the ass with him, that's what I'm attracted and addicted too.

"I believe you for some odd reason, Malik. What the fuck are you trying to do to me? You want me to be a fool for you?" I sighed. Malik backed me into the corner of our room. His lips and my lips touched each other. I love the way the weed smelled on his breath.

"Believe me baby, because it's true. I want to be a fool for you too Leah. I'm following your lead, but I don't know how much longer I can do that. I'm being patient as fuck. My old lady always told me good things comes to those who wait."

Chapter 13

Vell

Touch down. A nigga finally landed in Houston. We got in late last night. OG Roy wanted to go to the strip club. I told that nigga we were here on business and not pleasure. I haven't been out on the town in a minute. I've been busy handling business, stacking the blue faces like my life depended on it. I swore I was about to chill for the weekend. We had four shipments that came in this week. I was tired as fuck, but the money was coming in so fast I could barely keep count.

Our product was in high demand, so we were expanding. We had to feed the streets. I was addicted to fast cash, but we're making millions a week. I haven't had any sleep in a few days. I didn't even get the chance to get my dreads twisted before I left. Fuck that, I'll handle it when I get back home. It's some shit in Houston that was begging for my attention. Leah didn't send for me, but she knew she was going against the grain.

She knew Zo was going to sell her out. That's my nigga. What the fuck did she expect. As soon as I stepped off the plane and my feet hit the pavement. The fresh air hit my face. I knew I changed the forecast. I was on go and Leah was about to feel me. I was already on my chopped and screwed shit and I ain't talking about the fuckin' music. I'm going to chop this nigga and screw the fuck out of Leah's disrespectful ass. It felt good to change the forecast and I'm on my good bull shit. I'm going to hurt Leah's ass for real. I wish she stops playing with me.

I love the fuck out of Leah. She got me out in the streets to doing some crazy ass shit to prove my love and loyalty to her. I won't allow her to be with another man. Every time I step foot in the city, I was on some real wild west shit. As soon as we landed Zo was waiting on us. I slapped hands with my nigga. I was ready to get down to fuckin' business. It's too bad a nigga was here for business and not pleasure. Leah Marie was the only focus. Zo pulled off in traffic.

"Zo who is this nigga, tell me everything I need to know about him? I know you got something for me. What's up with the niggas you know out here?" I asked. I needed the rundown on this nigga because every nigga in my city knew Leah was mine and if they decided to go against the grain then we have an issue and I'll send their mother a box of fuckin' tissue."

"He goes by the name of Street, but his government is Malik Devereaux. I don't know if you know him or not, but he used to bang and get money with Skull and Veno. It's personal for me because when you use gang bang real tough, I killed both of his niggas on some real hot shit. He was in the car with them nigga. I busted at that nigga five times and he still didn't die. You know our motto is no face no case.

Nobody knew I killed those niggas not even Juelz and Skeet. Just in case he's on some get back shit because of his niggas, I was willing to kill him just off the strength of the shit that happened in 2005." He's knee deep in the streets too, he uses that Top Golf shit as a cover up. He's a little older than us, but them niggas ran the Southside. Sphinx, you remember Griff? He got killed a few months ago off Glenwood. That was his connect." He argued. I respect ZO for keeping it real about the shit he did. I knew of Griff. Them young niggas caught his ass slipping. I heard he took a few of them with him. We crossed paths a few times. I saw that shit on the news. I don't care what type of rank this nigga got. If I asked about him. I sure he's asked about me too.

"Fuck that nigga and his niggas. So, tell me about these niggas who know some niggas. Can I use these niggas and then kill them because niggas talk? Loose lips sink ships, how do you want to play this shit. I got enough muscle." I asked. Sphinx immediately cut me off.

"No offense ZO but we got enough muscle. Fuck them, niggas. Niggas talk too much and I'm trying to get back home to wife and kids. We just need the drop on Leah and ole boy and we can take it from there." He argued. Sphinx was really trying to get home.

"They're staying at our hotel, but we can't get at them there. It's too many fuckin' cameras. The street is sewed up and the hotel and security are deep as fuck. We have to catch them when they're moving." He explained. I agreed with Alonzo. Leah likes to be out on the scene and post up and shit. It wouldn't be hard to catch her.

"Vell, you dragged me to Houston to chase a chick. I tell you one thing young bull; this shit better be worth it. I'm not coming out of retirement for anything. I'm wetting the city up and I want to get my dick wet. Sphinx what's up with Helene. Shit, she got a man or what? If so, call her ass now and let her know Santa Claus is coming to town, put that nigga out for a few days. I want to play. I hope y'all told her about OG Roy. I bred you young bulls." Alonzo and Sphinx looked at me and laughed. Who told OG Roy about Helene.

"Calm down OG, we're going to pull up over there in a few minutes, she's cooking us some breakfast. Look, OG Roy, when we pull up at her house, act like you got some fuckin' sense. I mean that shit. She agreed to help us, don't fuck this shit up. We need her to drive while we're letting our guns loose." I argued. OG Roy is an aggressive ass nigga. Shit, he'll fuck around and run Helene off with his wild ass.

"Young Bull, OG Vell you better put some fuckin' respect on my name and act like you know. I know how to act around a woman and treat her right. You called me to track down your woman way out here in Texas."

"Yeah whatever, you heard what I said."

It was still early in the morning, I was hungry as fuck, and I haven't had any sleep. We pulled up at Helene's house. OG Roy was the first motherfucka out the door. Gawd damn he hasn't listened to shit I said. Zo and Sphinx were laughing their ass' off. They knew OG Roy was a gawd damn fool. Sphinx rang the doorbell. Helene opened the door and we entered the door the aroma of sausage, eggs, and grits hit my nostrils. I was ready to eat. I knew she was about to light a fire in our ass. We gave her a hug as we entered her home.

"Get y'all motherfuckin asses up in here. It's been a long time coming. Sphinx, you've been acting funny since you married Malone. Alonzo you know I wasn't fond of you and that gawd damn Alexis, but you love that big booty heifer, so it is what it is. Vell what the fuck is up with you and Leah? I'm sick of y'all shit. I thought y'all would've been back together by now. You did your shit and she did her shit too. I'm riding with my niggas right or wrong. What brings y'all to my neck of the woods? Who is this nigga y'all brought with y'all? He eye fucked me as if he knows me?

Does he know me or what? Introduce yourself. I'm Queen Helene and who the fuck are you?" She asked. Helene was off the hook. Her mouth was fly as fuck and she was jazzy with it. She had no clue he was loving all that shit. She was his type of woman. OG Roy started rubbing his goatee. Oh, hell nah, I knew he was up to no good. I told him to act like he got some sense. He wasn't going to act right.

"I'm OG Roy. I bred these two young bulls right here. Excuse me for my recklessness. I didn't mean to come in to your place without introducing myself. I didn't mean to grab you up either, but I didn't see an OG like myself in your vicinity. I'm a fresh ass bull and I'm intrigued by you. You're fine as hell. I should slap the shit out of my nephews for keeping you a secret. You're showing all these young bulls some love. Show OG Roy some love too." He stated. OG Roy felt up Helene. Sphinx and Vell looked at me and we busted out laughing.

"Gawd damn OG motherfuckin Roy. You're my type of nigga. I'm feeling that fly as shit you just spit. Where are you staying at tonight? You and I might be able to get in a little trouble." She stated, she was sizing him up. I done

fucked up. I shouldn't have brought his ass. I need Helene
to ride with us on some real hot shit.

"I can stay with you if you want me too." He explained.
Damn, can he let her go?

"You for damn sure can," she sassed.

"Hey before y'all two hook-up we need to get down to
business," I argued.

"Come on and let me feed y'all. Vell it's too early to be
the fuckin' grinch. Don't come up in my house giving
fuckin' orders. I'm a grown ass motherfuckin' woman. I
got needs too, just like y'all motherfuckas do. Sit your ass
down and eat. I didn't tell you to cheat. I'm all for your
good bull shit but right is right and wrong is wrong." She
argued and laughed. Helene fixed all our plates. This food
was good as hell too. OG Roy pulled Helene on his lap. She
started feeding him and he was loving that shit. It's a wrap
now. That's all he needed was a woman and he was done.

"Helene, Leah is out here with another man being really
disrespectful. I got to handle my business. Tonight, I got
plans to murk that nigga. I need a driver and you're my
rider. I'm throwing you the keys. It's hunting season. Leah
is my prey and that nigga is my target." I explained.

"Oh really, that heifer came to my city and didn't pull up? Where can we find her ass at? She knows I don't play that disrespectful as shit when it comes to my niggas. What you need me to do? If you want me to shoot, I'll shoot that nigga. If you want me to set it up, run me the fuckin' play. Don't spare that pussy ass nigga when it comes to the woman you love. Show that nigga how you fuckin' give it up. I have connections. This is my city. I got a few niggas who work for the Houston Police Department.

If you need any bodies bagged and moved, they'll clean up that shit. I'll just have to make the call. I got a few niggas who work for the State Patrol. They'll shut down I-10 if we need them too. If that nigga wants a war, we'll shoot it out and clear the fuckin' smoke. What do you want to do OG Vell? I'm riding with you." Helene ain't said nothing but a thing. She already knew what time it was. My rider was on go for show. We finished chopping it up with Helene. I tried to get OG Roy to bust a move with us, but he wasn't leaving this place.

I had so much fuckin' energy. I knew Leah was the air I breathed. Sphinx and I rented a loft in the city. I couldn't stay at the same hotel they were staying at because

I would murk that nigga on site for flaunting what's mine on his arms. I would be facing some major fuckin' time. I would have to flee the country. Those pussy ass crackers would have to kill me. I wasn't going out like that. I would pull the same shit my OG did.

I was stalking Leah's IG. She knew not to post that nigga or her whereabouts. I can't wait to get this shit over with and bring her ass home. She got me so fucked up. I'm feeding off her energy. Sphinx was on the phone caking with Malone. My OG has been on me tough these past few weeks. She knew I was up to no good. She called me a few times this week and I didn't answer. She just called my phone and I didn't answer. It's hunting season and nobody's going to stop me from doing that.

"Aye Vell momma is trying to call you, answer your fuckin' phone," he yelled. My mother called my phone back. I had to answer because Sphinx confirmed that we were together.

"Hey ma what's up? Is everything okay?" I asked. I had to play shit cool because my mother knew me better than I knew myself.

"Everything is good on my end. I've been trying to reach you for a few days and you haven't returned any of my calls. I never had to go through Sphinx to get you on the phone. So, what's up? What's going on in Houston? I called Roy to see what was up. I sent some packages to the spot and nobody was there to sign for them. I'm trying to see whose handling my fuckin' business if you're in Houston?" She asked. My mother was trying to run game. I had Layla pick the pack up.

"Ma the package was picked up. Business is business. I'm sure you check the numbers as much as I do. I didn't know it was a crime to take a vacation."

"If you're on vacation how come Malone and Leah aren't with you?" She asked.

"Ma, I have another call coming in. Let me call you right back." I laughed.

"Yeah, you do that. I need to have a serious fuckin' talk with you and Leah. LaVell you're hard headed. Don't make a mess that you can't clean up." She argued and sassed. If she knew what I was up to, why call and ask? I wasn't calling her back until I got back home. I laid back on my bed and scrolled through Instagram. Leah posted a thirst trap she was headed to. Onyx. I started to reply see you soon. I rubbed my hands together like birdman. Too bad I wouldn't be able to enjoy those strippers tonight. Leah was the only one I wanted to bust it open. These bitches can't do shit out here for me. I ain't got no rap for them.

I got the drop on Leah. I was an impatient ass nigga. We pulled up at Onyx early. I wanted to get a section, so I could get a full view of the club. I couldn't even enjoy myself because Leah was heavy on my mind. I never thought I would be doing this shit right here, but when you love somebody you to take drastic measures. We had plenty of bitches in our section. Zo and Sphinx were both curving these hoes. I just paid them to dance. Leah was my focus. OG Roy and Helene were posted by the bar. I didn't want Leah to see Helene because she would've known I was in here. The moment her and old boy made it inside, Roy hit my line and said we had company. I ain't never caught Leah with this nigga but I wanted to see her in action. I stood up and scanned the club for her.

They were posted up at the bar. I can spot Leah from anywhere. I didn't like the way that nigga looked at her and the way she looked at him. It was showtime. I watched Leah and that nigga for a few minutes.

I was ready to get this shit over with and get these pussy whipped niggas back to their wives. I had to make sure my first move was my best move. I'm a wild ass nigga, but I calculate shit too.

I saw enough and exited our VIP Section. Sphinx grabbed my shoulder and I brushed him off. "I got this shit nigga, just cover me in case a nigga acts ignorant." Sphinx and Zo followed suit. Yeah, we were in a club, but I only had two targets, Leah and that sucka ass nigga that thinks he's about to be with her. It's not going down like that at all. I approached Leah. I stood behind her and I grabbed her hand. I was marking my territory. She knew she couldn't pull this shit in Atlanta. She turned around and looked at me with a scowl on her face. She might as well turn that shit into a frown.

"What's up Leah Marie Baptiste, you're disrespectful as fuck. I told you about that shit. I make good on all my promises. Let's roll, it's time to bring your ass home and it ain't up for debate." I argued.

"Vell, why are you here? I'm not trying to do this shit here with you. I want you to leave me alone." She argued. Ole boy turned around. She knows why I'm here.

"I'm here because of you Leah. It ain't no breaking up. I don't give two fucks about where we're at." I argued. "You know what it is with me."

"No disrespect Vell, but you're on my fuckin' time. You need to move around lil buddy." He argued and snarled his face. That tough shit didn't scare me. I laughed at his pussy ass. I'm glad he made that move. I was ready to make mine.

"Aye NIGGA, this is shit me, and what Leah got going on ain't got shit to do with you, my nigga. If it's an issue and you want to get involved, let a nigga know something? I'll be glad to solve any fuckin' problem that you have. I got a few myself." I heard the Glock pull back and go click clack. I know that was Zo or Sphinx. Sphinx passed me the strap quick and I pointed it at that nigga's head. "What the fuck was you saying again? You got three seconds or else I'm letting this bitch rip. I warned you to stay the fuck up out of my business. Are you hard of hearing? Leah and I got relations. Our shit is deeper than this little front she's putting on with you." I argued. I don't give a fuck about airing this nigga out in broad daylight.

"Aye, nigga you ain't the only one holding. Let me defend myself and we can shoot out properly. May the best man win." He argued. He pushed Leah behind him and he pulled out his strap. Everybody was running out of the club. Sphinx and Zo had their guns pointed at this nigga too.

"Leah you need to come on before you get this man killed. Act like you motherfuckin' know. We're not playing with a full deck. If my nephew pulled up, it wasn't on a friendly fuckin' visit. Don't sign this niggas death certificate if you don't have too." Helene argued and explained. She had her gun pointed at the back of ole boy's head. She was trained to go.

"Come on Vell, let's go because you don't even have to do all of this shit to prove a point. Put the gun down your issue is with me, not him. He doesn't have shit to do with what we have going on. Malik and I didn't meet off the strength of me getting back at you. I'm single and he's single." She argued. Leah grabbed my hand pulling me away. Sphinx, Zo and Helene still had their gun trained on him.

"Leah where the fuck are you going," he argued and snarled his face up at us. He was making his way toward Leah. He made the wrong fuckin' move.

"Don't say shit Leah, you know what time it is. You made the right fuckin' move. This shit is between he and I.

I told you to stay the fuck up out of my business. You see she's leaving with me." I argued. "She made her fuckin' decision and it ain't you my nigga."

"Vell, come on, please. Put the gun down. You asked me to leave and I'm fuckin' leaving. I'm doing what you asked me to do. Can you do what the fuck I asked you too?" She argued and cried. I did what Leah asked me to do. I walked out of the club with my eyes trained on ole boy. A nigga can never get at me with my back turned. Leah got in the car and slammed the door.

"Aye Vell, circle back around the block. I got to handle some shit really quick." Sphinx yelled. I knew what that meant. Zo climbed in the back. OG Roy and Helene were following us.

"Where too?" The driver asked.

"Hobby." Leah was still crying. "I don't know what the fuck you're crying for, I didn't even get the chance to kill the nigga. All this shit could've been avoided if you would've done what I asked." I ain't never pulled a gun out on a nigga and didn't use it. I'll see that nigga again.

Chapter-14

Sphinx

If I was called on a mission. I didn't come out here just to bring Leah home and dip. I was under the impression Vell was gone murk a nigga. He wants to call everybody pussy whipped except his motherfuckin' self. Leah got that nigga gone. I ain't never known that nigga not to kill anything. Leah didn't want that nigga to die because she still had plans to be with him. I saw through all that shit. I had to handle the mission and my fuckin' business. It ain't no other way. It's always no face no case with me.

I ain't leaving shit unturned. Ole boy that Leah was with he had a lot of heart and I respect that. It was just too bad that tonight would be the last time that motherfucka pumps. I wouldn't let that nigga live another day to come back and hunt us. It ain't going down like that. Leah was making sure that Vell didn't kill that nigga. He didn't have too, but I would. I had to get at him. I calculated this play to perfection. I knew how I wanted to play this shit. Leah was feeling this nigga too. I could see it in his face and hers too. My OG had a problem on his hands. It's all good. I'm the nigga to deal with the problems.

I'm my brother's keeper. I live by and die by that shit. I was always two steps ahead of motherfuckas. Vell went to sleep earlier. Something told me to move around and check shit out. I dipped off back to the hotel that ole boy and Leah was staying at. I wanted to see what type of car that nigga was driving. I sat in the parking lot for a minute. They finally pulled up and Leah had a shit load of bags. I could tell he was feeling her.

He looked at her the same way Vell did. Too bad for him Leah was already taken and Vell planned to keep it that way. Ole boy was slick. He had two cars at the hotel. They were both parked right beside each other. He threw a bag in the other one. As soon as they walked in. I got out and put a tracker underneath each car. I checked my phone and his car was still in the parking lot. Music to my ears. That nigga was probably somewhere plotting. It's too bad it's a killer on the loose.

Vell could look Leah in the face and admit to not killing her little friend to pacify her feelings. I didn't have to do that. My wife already knew what it was with me. I had my Ski-mask tucked in my pocket already. I pulled out my black gloves from my back pocket. Ole boy was walking to his car. He didn't see me behind him when I ran up on him. I had my Mac 11 cocked and ready. He was on the phone running his mouth, not paying attention to his surroundings.

"Aye, I need the rundown on that nigga Vell. He just pulled down on me with Zo and another nigga, they looked like twins. I owe Zo one anyway for the shit he pulled with Skull and Veno. I've let that nigga slide one too many fuckin' times. It's time to dead that shit. A nigga can't draw down on me with a gun and not use that motherfucka. I'm from the nine and I don't give a fuck about dying. Pull up at Onyx, them niggas can't be too far." He argued and yelled through the phone. No face no case. I knew it. It's too bad I beat that nigga at his own game. My game. I tapped him on his shoulder. He turned around and looked at me. I pulled my ski-mask off I wanted him to look in the eyes of his killer.

"I heard you were looking for me pussy ass nigga?" He was looking scared as shit. Just a few minutes ago he was running his mouth about drawing down on me. I shot his pussy ass dead in his head and he dropped to the ground. I shot his ass in the head again to make sure he was dead. Motherfuckas that get shot in the head can survive too. I kneeled to check his pulse. He didn't have one. I blew the whistle for OG Roy and Helene pulled up. They pulled up in a black Crown Vic with tinted windows.

"Get rid of this shit. Can you two handle it?" I argued.

"Yeah, what the fuck do you think?" OG Roy was trying to impress Helene. I'm not beat for his shit. I sent Vell a text and told him to pull back up. He sent a text back and said that he was on his way. OG Roy and I lifted ole boy's body in the back of the trunk. OG Roy doused the trunk with gasoline.

"Make sure this shit never comes back. Handle this before you and Helene take it in. Where do you want us to pick you up from?" I asked.

"I'm staying out here for a few days. I'll see you in the hood." He stated. I slapped hands with OG Roy. I walked back toward the front.

Vell was waiting for me. Leah was sitting up front with a frown on her face. I hopped in and the driver pulled off. Vell looked at me, trying to read my facial expression. No words were spoken between us. Now I was ready to leave Houston.

Leah

I couldn't stop the tears from falling. I buried my face in my hands. My pants where soaked. I didn't give a damn about Sphinx being in the car with us. I was in my feelings. Vell wouldn't let me be great. I was so uncomfortable in the car with Sphinx and Vell as we headed to the airport. I had so much shit I wanted to say to Vell, but Sphinx didn't need to hear it. I had a lot on my chest and I wanted to get it off. To make matters worse Queen Helene was supposed to be on my fuckin' side and have my back. She flipped the script on me. I could've shitted bricks when she started popping slick at the mouth. I couldn't wait to tell Malone and Layla how she showed her ass pulling a gun out on my man with OG Roy.

I ain't surprised she's riding with the two of them. No matter what, they can do no wrong in her eyes. I was the victim. He cheated on me and I didn't even get to cheat back. I thought she was supposed to be supporting me, but she's riding with her fuckin' nephews community dick ass. I knew Vell was going to kill Malik. I couldn't let him do that. What hurts the most is how Malik looked at me. He was disgusted and that shit hurts because we were better than that. I couldn't let him die. I care about that man so much. I know he cares about me too. I couldn't let him lose his life. He deserves to be happy even if it's not with me.

I couldn't even look at Vell when we got on the plane. He knew he was wrong. Malik wasn't backing down and I love that about him. When he pushed me behind him, I knew it was on. Alonzo ain't shit. He's always in somebody else's fuckin' business. I can't wait to talk to Alexis about his ass. I can't stand him. Vell took a seat next to me on the plane.

"Why are you crying, Leah?" He asked. He knew why I was upset.

"I don't want to talk about it here Vell," I argued and sobbed. Our plane took off. He grabbed my hand and I snatched it away from him. He grabbed it again and slid my engagement ring back on my finger.

"Don't take that motherfucka off Leah I'm not playing. I'm sorry. I love you, Leah. I just want to cuff you." He explained. How does he go from being aggressive to being nice?

Chapter-15

Sphinx

Leah and Vell wore me out. It hurt my heart to hear Leah cry. Instantly I thought about my wife. I hate to hear Malone cry especially when it's because of me. I have three daughters and I don't ever want a man to make them cry. Vell loves Leah and he needs to get his shit together and let that hoe shit go. He's changed. These hoes ain't worth it. He sees that shit for what it is. I know he really loves Leah because he didn't murder that nigga.

A nigga like me I didn't come to Houston to leave without a body. I don't give a fuck how much Malone begged me not to a kill a nigga I wouldn't do it. She knows me better than that. I'm a natural born killer. More of the reason why I stayed behind to handle my brother's fuckin' business. I saw the look in that nigga's eyes. I knew he would come for Vell. Not while I was living. He couldn't live amongst us. Any threat to my brother is a threat to me. As soon as we stepped foot on the jet. I took a seat ducked off in the back. I couldn't wait to make it home to my wife. I swear this was probably going to be the longest hour and fifty-five minutes ever. I knew sleep wouldn't take me over because I was too anxious to get home.

As soon as our flight landed, and I felt the jet's wheels touch the pavement it was on, fuck the safe landing. I snatched my seatbelt off. I didn't even tell Vell bye. I had to make it home. Malone was the only thing on my mind. It was a little after 3:00 a.m. I knew Malone was sleeping. I had plans to wake her up. I had to check on my babies first. I knew Jah would hold it down. Samaya and Kennedy were knocked out asleep. I checked on the twins, and they were asleep.

I sat my duffel bag on the floor and pulled the covers back. Malone started stirring in her sleep. She was naked as the day she was born. My dick got hard instantly. I came up out of my clothes quick. "Daddy's home." I threw her legs over my shoulders. Malone was thick as fuck too. My babies put the pound game to her. I started tongue fucking her pussy. I missed her.

It didn't take her long to wake up and start feeding me. I could tell she missed me too. She started riding my face as her life depended on it. She was pulling my dreads and I knew she was about to cum.

"Throw that pussy like you missed me, Malone." She did as she was told. I wanted to catch all of that. Her juices rained down on my face. I slurped all that up.

As soon as I felt her body jerk. I knew she had gotten hers. It was time for me to put in overtime and get mine. I raised up from between her legs. She wrapped her arms around my neck and started kissing me. I guess she missed me after she cursed my ass out.

"I missed you. Why you didn't tell me you were coming back home tonight? I would've waited up on you," she asked? I didn't want her waiting up on me. She needed to get as much rest as possible since she didn't have any help with the kids today.

"I wanted to surprise you and to beat this pussy up. I missed the fuck out of you. I told you I would wake you up when I came back and that's what I intended to do. I missed you, Malone."

"I missed you too." She was biting her bottom lip. Malone grabbed my dick with her free hand and started stroking it. My dick was already hard. I didn't need any help. The only help I needed was for her to open her legs.

"Let me taste you? I want to taste you." She asked. Malone wanted to take control and tonight that shit wasn't happening.

"I don't want you to taste me. I'm trying to please you." I argued. I was in charge tonight and I wanted her to follow my lead. I started at the top and I wanted to work my way to the bottom. Malone smelled good as fuck. Leah probably told her we were on the way. I sucked the right side of her neck. "I want my name tatted right here."

"Okay." She moaned. Her neck was covered in my bite marks. Her nipples were extra hard begging for me to suck them. I ran my tongue across each one of them. I had to be careful with sucking them, breast milk might start leaking. I threw her legs over my shoulder and placed her ass on the bottom of my knees. I was ready to dive deep off in this pussy. Malone tried to raise up. I smacked her on the ass.

"Be still and let me do what the fuck I'm trying to do," I argued. My dick wasn't even all the way in before she started moaning and squirming. She better takes this dick because I was taking this pussy.

"It hurts." She moaned and whined. I ignored her. I stroked her long, deep, and hard. I was putting in work. I was pounding the fuck out of her pussy. The head board kept banging up against the wall, so I grabbed a pillow and put it in between. "Stop fuckin' moving Malone." The sweat from my forehead dripped on her stomach. Each time I slid out of her pussy, her juices were running out and sliding down the crack of her ass. We were making a baby tonight.

"Riiigghhtt there Sphinx," she moaned. I love the way her juices coated my dick. She started grinding on me and throwing her pussy back at me. I slapped her on her ass. I wanted her to be still, that's it.

"Did I tell you to move? Did I tell you to throw this pussy back?" I asked and grunted. She rolled her eyes at me and placed her hands on my shoulder. I politely moved her hands. She wanted to be hard headed, so she didn't need to hold on to me for support. "Squat and ride." She started riding my dick real wild and foolish. She was riding it like a pro. I rested my hands behind my head. I just stood in place and watched her do her thing. Fuck she was extra wet. Each time she would squat, she would squeeze her pussy muscles. She was gripping the fuck out of my dick. I felt like I was about to bust a nut. I could feel her pussy muscles clamp down on my dick when she was pulling me in. I wasn't ready to buss just yet. I flipped her over and told her about doing that shit.

"Let me hit it from the back. Face down ass up." She did as she was told. I smacked her on her ass a few times. I grabbed her hair and she grabbed the pillow for support. "Toot that ass up." My free hand was on her left ass cheek. I kept pounding her from the back with each stroke her ass jiggled. She kept running from the dick. She knew I was punishing her ass.

"Slow down it hurts Sphinx." She moaned and begged.

"Stop running from the dick Malone and it wouldn't hurt." I tightened my grip on her hair. She looked over her shoulders trying to look at me.

She had a few tears in the corner of her eyes. We were in sync with each other. For every long stroke, I gave her she gave me one. She kept watching me. I grabbed her face and tongued her down.

"I'm about to cum." She moaned. As soon as I felt her juices coat my dick I came too. I picked her up and carried her to the shower. She could barely stand up. I sat her on the bench in the shower while I cut the water on to our liking. I grabbed a towel and washed her face. I made sure the towel was extra soapy. I washed every inch of her body. I was tired as fuck and ready to lay it down.

"I love you, Lateef."

"You better. I love you too Malone, let me dry you off so we can go to sleep." I carried Malone to our room. I laid her across my chest and we drifted off to sleep. I was tired as fuck. I haven't had any sleep since I left home. I wasn't leaving the house for a few days.

Vell

Sphinx didn't even say bye to a nigga. I know he was headed home. That's the only place he wanted to be. I got to swing by the house tomorrow because we'll have to catch up. I know he did some shit that he hasn't spoken on. I need to make sure it was cleaned up properly. I ain't mad at him. I expected that from him. It was just Leah, me, and our pilot left. Leah was dragging her feet. I knew she was in her feelings but it's time for her to get out of them. I want to move on and start over. I grabbed her hand and led her to the car. I was surprised she didn't object.

"I didn't get to get my stuff Vell. I left a lot of stuff in Houston." She argued and sassed.

"I'll replace whatever you left." Leah and I hopped in the Wraith and pulled off.

"Where are we headed too," she asked.

"Home." I heard Leah huffing and puffing and mumbling some shit under her breath.

"I'm not going home with you Vell. You can take me to my house. You and I aren't that cool to be in the same space." She argued.

"Leah I'm sorry. I swear to God I am, and I'll forever tell you that until we can move on. I know you'll never forget but can you find it in your heart to forgive me. I'm just asking for one chance to make it right?" I asked.

"Vell, I forgive you, but I'll never forget. I'm tired of even discussing this shit. Every time we talk about us and what happened I get upset. I just want to know, why you don't want me to be happy? I want to know why you won't let me move on?" I had to pull over on the side of the road.

"Leah, I love you. Do you know that? I ain't never been in love before until I ran across you. I'm not trying to love anybody else but you. I want to work this out. It took everything in me not to kill that nigga. I spared him because you begged me not kill him. What I did was wrong, and I can't change that. I fucked up big time.

Can we start over? All I'm asking is for another chance? I don't want you happy if it's not with me. I'm the only man that can make you happy. Why are you trying to move on? We can work it out?"

"I don't know Vell. It's something that I'll have to think about? If I cheated on you? Would you forgive me and take me back? Would our love trump my infidelities?" She asked. Leah backed me in a hole with that one. "Answer me?"

"Did you fuck that nigga Leah?" I asked. I wanted to know because if she did. I'm going back to Houston to handle that.

"Answer my question Vell?" She asked.

"Answer mine first?"

"No, I didn't fuck him. I wanted too, but he didn't want to cross that line." She explained.

"Yeah I'll forgive, but it'll take some time."

"Okay that's all I'm asking for is time."

"How much time do you need?" Leah didn't even respond. She was coming home with me rather she wanted to or not.

Chapter-16

Leah

I love Malone to death. I swear to God I do. We've been best friends forever. I've never seen her this happy before. I'm glad she was able to experience that with Sphinx. However, I'm tired of coming to her house every Sunday and Vell is here. Ugh, and to think I use to love his trifling ass. To make matters worse he's always staring at me, trying to read my soul. I hate it no matter how intense the stare is. The pain is still here no matter how I portray myself on the outside. He was the cause, but I didn't want him to be the cure. We are done. That's the only thing I wanted him to understand. Even though time has passed I still can't forget it.

"Leah I'm so sick of you and Vell. I wish you two would kiss and make up already," she sassed and laughed. I rolled my eyes at her so fuckin' hard. Malone held Laylin in her arms and she was smiling so hard. You could tell she would be cutting teeth soon. I could see something white poking through her gums. Malone is probably pregnant again. Laylin looked exactly like her father. I told Malone about lying on her back and cocking her legs open for him. Malone was laughing so hard. Vell was looking over here at us. He drained the life out of my face. I couldn't even eat dinner, because he killed my appetite. Yeah, it was time for me to fuckin' go. I've been here too long.

"I'm sick of him too Malone. He can forget about any kissing or making up with me. I'll catch you later this week." I argued and sighed. I kissed Laylin on her cheek. I grabbed my coat and purse. I was ready to go hours ago. It was the beginning of the winter and it was cold outside. Malone and Sphinx's house was so big it sat on a lake. The wind mixed with cool water coming from the lake had me freezing. I walked to my car quickly. As soon as my hand touched the handle. I felt a pair of hands wrapped around my waist. Chills ran through my body. I knew it was Vell. I could smell his cologne and the liquor on his breath. We just stood in place for a few minutes. Vell's nose was cold. He had the tip snuggled against the crook of my neck.

"Can you please move?" I argued and sighed. Stop walking up on me.

"I don't want too." He spewed. He bit the side of my neck.

"Let me go Vell. I got to go." I argued. It's too cold outside to be fooling around with him.

"I'm sorry Leah. What a nigga got to do to make shit right with us Leah. I'm out here going crazy without you. I want to come back home. I miss the shit out of you Leah. My life hasn't been right since I fucked up." He begged and pleaded. I swear Vell makes this shit so hard, but I'm standing my ground. It's not easy getting back in my good graces. Especially after he fucked up.

"I miss you to Vell more than you would ever know. You'll have to learn to live your life without me. You cheated and lied. We're in this space because of you. You had me out here looking like a fool, and you thought you could play me. You think I wanted this? Vell, we were supposed to get married. You got all these bitches out here laughing at me. I thought you were different Vell, but I should've known better.

It's my fault I should've stayed single and played you how you played me. A nigga ain't never hurt me before, as soon as I let you in and started fucking with you heavy, you hurt me. I had doubts for the longest and decided to give this love thing a try. I let you cuff me Vell and you fucked up. Damn all I wanted was you. In the beginning, you were perfect. Now I'm in my feelings and I'm living in hell. Looking for a way out." I argued and cried. I didn't even notice the tears started falling.

"Leah I can't change the past, but every bitch that laughed at you because of me, I'll leave them lifeless. I put that shit on my OG. Baby, I'm sorry. I swear to God I am. Can I prove it to you? Can I right every wrong. Let me love the hurt out of your heart," He pleaded. It's getting late and I'm freezing.

"I got to go Vell it's cold and it was good seeing you. I can't even get over you because you're always bringing this up" I tried to break free from his grasp, but he had a hold on me so tight. I couldn't bust a move. I'm trying to make it home before it started snowing, and now they're starting to fall.

"Come on Leah, ride with me. Please don't leave. Can you forgive me, please? You don't have to forget. This is my second time asking you. Meet me halfway. I want to fix this and fix us. I swear to God I'm trying. I want my family back. Can I please have it back? You come first, and the streets will come second." He begged and pleaded. Vell was really trying to wear me down.

"Why should I Vell?" I asked. I wanted to know.

"Take a ride with me and see please?" He asked.

"Why do I have to ride with you to find out?"

"Because it's cold out here and I don't want you to get sick? Can I have a few hours of your time?" He asked.

"Not tonight Vell. I'll see you around." He finally let me free of his embrace. I tried to get in my car. He grabbed my hand. I looked over my shoulder to see what he wanted. He gave me a kiss. I didn't kiss him back.

"I love you, Leah." I didn't even respond. I got in my car and pulled off as fast as I could. I had to stay far away from Vell. Something was telling me to ride with him, but I wasn't ready for that. My heart was saying yes but my mind was saying hell no. Vell and I haven't had a real conversation since Houston. I wish he would leave me alone. Malone called my phone and the Bluetooth connected immediately.

"What's up, Malone? I'm not coming to your house anymore."

"Why? I saw you booed up with Vell outside on the cameras. I swear that was the cutest thing ever. The snow was falling and shit. Girl, I feel bad for Vell. My heart hurts for him. Girl you're taking his ass down through there." She laughed.

"Fuck you, Malone, you're always taking up for him. I'll talk to you tomorrow I'm going to find myself. Maybe I'll run into Malik."

"Girl stay away from him. Call me tomorrow." Malone hung up the phone and I cut the music up.

Chapter-17

Malone

I swear I didn't mean to run Leah off. I love my best friend to death and I want to see her happy again even if it's not with Vell, but I prefer them together because they balance each other out. I know OG Vell can make that happen. Leah is set in her ways and once you cross her one time, it ain't no coming back from that. I put Laylin and Lateef both down. Neither of them didn't feel good. I gave them baths. Laylin went right to bed. She was teething bad and extra whinny for no reason.

Sphinx was watching a movie with Jah, Kennedy, and Samaya. Lateef wanted me to hold him all night. I don't know who was worse him or his father. Sphinx hates that he's so spoiled. What the fuck does he expect? That's what you do with babies. You spoil them. I heard our room door open. I looked up and it was Sphinx. I cracked a smile at him because I knew he was about to say something smart.

"Malone what did I tell you about holding him all the time?" He argued. I knew it.

"Sphinx shut up, he's a baby, my baby and he doesn't feel good, so he needs a little bit more attention." I sassed. Lateef was smiling at me because I was giving his father the business. Sphinx climbed in the bed beside me and started biting my neck.

"Stop Sphinx," I moaned.

"Daddy needs some attention too." Sphinx grabbed Lateef out of my hands. I rolled my eyes at him.

"Don't do that Malone. I'm taking him to his room." He smiled. I can't stand his petty ass. Sphinx phone started ringing. Who the fuck is calling my husband's phone this time of night? I grabbed his phone and answered it.

"Hello." I sassed. I had so much base in my voice I knew a bitch could feel it.

"Put my baby daddy on the phone," she sassed and sucked her teeth. I looked at the phone as if she could see me. Mesha had a problem, and I'm the bitch to solve it. I don't give a fuck if Sphinx is your baby daddy or not, he's my husband and its fucking boundaries. I'm here to set them.

"My husband is busy, so how can I help you?" I argued. I was giving her the same energy she was giving me.

"Tell MY BABY DADDY OUR SON doesn't feel good and I don't have a car to take him to the hospital. THANKS TO YOU. I need a ride to urgent care. He needs to bring his ASS and that long, thick, black dick that WE all love so much," she laughed. Oh, this bitch was trying me. I'm here for it.

"Too bad I'm his WIFE. I'm the only woman that's riding that BIG BLACK, LONG THICK DICK that hoes loves but can't even get close to it. I hit HIGH NOTES when I'm singing my solo on it. Sphinx touch the back of my throat. I'm his Queen, the one you chicks love to hate. Mesha you can't compete, because you can NEVER compare to me.

Try again bitch because I got motherfuckin time." I laughed. She hung up the phone. I'm saying though, these bitches don't want to fuck with me behind my husband. A bitch will get shot dead in their head. I'm just being honest.

"Malone, who the fuck is you in here talking too like that? I want to feel that high note you were bragging about. Let me coach you with an acappella." He laughed. I can't stand his cocky ass, but I can't get enough of him.

"Your baby momma was testing my gangster. Latwoin is supposed to be sick. I'll head over there and pick him up."

"Malone, it's too late for you to be out by yourself without me," he argued. I don't give a fuck what Sphinx is talking about. I'm going. I threw on my black Calvin Klein sweat suit on and my black Timberland boots. I guarantee you I'm going to stomp a bitch out today. I feel like Kirk Franklin in this bitch. STOMP.

Oh, oh, oh, oh,

Stomp on the enemy cause I've got the victory

Mesha can get it today. I got nothing but time.

"Malone do you hear me fuckin' talking to you?" He yelled. Sphinx knows when he hollers at me it turns me on. Right now, I'm not listening.

"I hear you Sphinx but I'm still going, because you're not about to go to no woman's house at 11:00 p.m. at night. I don't give a fuck who it is. I know she wants to fuck you. I just want to see how bad. You can ride with me or you can get the fuck out my way, Mr. Baptiste." I argued. Sphinx knows that once my mind is made up. It ain't no stopping me.

He walked up behind me and wrapped his arms around my waist. He started kissing me on my neck and fondling with my breast.

"Calm down Malone. Do you trust me?" He asked. I tilted my neck back and gazed into his eyes.

"Of course, I trust you, but I know these hoes. I know a hoe can't wait to sink their claws into you. You know I'm not having that shit. She can get a ride everywhere else, but not to Urgent Care to see about my son? Bitches got shit confused Sphinx. He's been sick all day? Get the fuck out of here. You need to get custody of him too. One less bitch I have to check about my child and not treating him properly, but always got her hand out."

"I hear you, Mrs. Baptiste." Sphinx was putting on his clothes right behind me. My Auntie Linda Faye moved in with us to help us out with the kids. I told her to keep an eye on the kids while we step out for a minute. Sphinx opened the car door for me and I slid in the peanut butter seats. He grabbed my thigh and my hands and kissed it. I looked at him out the corner of my eye and smiled. I love me some him.

"I love your mean ass, Malone. These bitches ain't got nothing on you," he laughed.

"Oh, I know, you put a ring on it didn't you." I laughed.

"I sure did. What the fuck you thought this was? I wore you down girl, you know you wanted me. You couldn't get enough of me. Once you gave me head it was a wrap.

The moment I dived in the pussy, you signed your death and marriage certificate. A nigga almost drowned, but I came back with that, death stroke and murdered the fuck out of that pussy. I put my name on all of that. I buried two seeds deep in it." He laughed. Sphinx grabbed my pussy. I swear Sphinx is full of shit, but what I can say is, he makes me so happy and he keeps a smile on my face. I couldn't ask for a better husband. He's perfect and I love him so much. Just the thought of him brings a smile to my face.

"What the fuck are you over there smiling about," he asked?

"Wouldn't you like to know," I snickered and smiled.

"Malone stop fucking playing with me?" He argued. Sphinx had his face turned up. He knew he had all my heart.

Sphinx

Malone is crazier than a motherfucka. I've rubbed off on my wife. I thought I was tripping for a minute. I heard her in our room popping off while I was putting our son to sleep. Mesha was tripping and on some good bull shit. She pulled up to the funeral home earlier today asking for some money for Latwoin. I told her no. Whatever he needs I always buy it, she called herself popping up at my place of business and I yanked her ass up and choked her ass the fuck out. Malone checked her ass. She needed too. She knows better than to call my house at 11:00 p.m.

If my son was sick, she could've called me earlier and I could've handled that. Malone and I pulled up at Mesha's house. Before I could even throw the car in park my wife was hopping out. She was on one and Mesha was liable to get it. I could hear Malone banging on Mesha's door like she was the police. I rested my head on the steering wheel. Malone was yelling my name. "Sphinx I knew this chick was on some good bull shit. Latwoin isn't here. Since I made a house call, I'm going to go ahead and whoop her ass, since I'm here," she yelled. I jumped out the car without even closing the door and taking my key out the ignition. It was too late. Malone had Mesha on the ground tagging her ass.

Mesha had on a little ass lingerie piece. I'm not even thinking about her ass. The only woman I wanted to look at was my wife. I scooped my wife up and threw her over my shoulders and carried her to the car. "Call my husband's phone again at 11:00 p.m. on some bullshit. I guarantee you I'll make you eat cow shit and you won't live to gossip to them bitches about it. Keep trying me. I'm so gone off my husband I can't wait to shoot a bitch," she spat. What the fuck am I going to do with her? She's too wild. I placed her on her feet and wrapped my arms around her.

"Malone, why are you out here showing out? Baby you don't have to do any of this shit. This ain't even you. I didn't marry you for this. I love you just the way you are. I'm not trying to change you, but you changed me and I'm forever grateful for you.

I thank God every day for placing you in my life and making you my wife. I don't want you out here wilding out." I pleaded and explained.

"I know Sphinx, but she tried it. She used Latwoin as an excuse for you to come through. She was trying to fuck you," she argued.

"Malone Baptiste, you're the only woman that carries my last name besides my daughters. I wanted you to be my wife the moment I met you. I was determined for you to be mine. You belong to me. You're the woman I want riding my dick. Another woman can't do anything for me because you do everything for me. My heart beats for you. This dick between my legs, it only gets hard for you. Malone you know I only want you.

I went through a lot just to get you and reach this point. I will never fuck shit up between us because I can't lose you. I'm not trying to live my life without you." I cupped her chin forcing her to look at me.

"I hear you Lateef. I love you too with all my heart. All that shit better be true," she sighed and cracked a faint smile.

"You're on punishment when we get home. You can't be out here showing your ass just because. I can't wait to get home and tear your mean ass up. You won't be able to walk for a few days.

"No Sphinx I'm own my cycle," she lied. Malone was pregnant she's been extra wet. I've been wondering when she's going to tell me.

"Malone you've never been good at lying to me. I know your body better than you do. I'm a gynecologist and I specialize in Malone Baptiste. Your cycle hasn't come this month. Are we having another baby or not? It's the only way I'm taking it easy on that pussy tonight?" Malone bit her bottom lip. I knew she was pregnant.

Chapter 18

Leah

"I love Vell to death. Hands up I can't lie. I'm going to love him until I die. It was easy to leave him, but no matter how hard I tried. He wouldn't ease up, he would never let me be. I changed and Vell has changed too. We changed and that could be a good thing or a bad thing. I'm ready for this storm to pass. It's been brewing for so long I'm just ready for it to be over. I have strong feelings for Malik too. I care about him. My heart hurts for him. My heart is really hurting behind what happened in Houston. I wish things would've played out differently, but they didn't. I hate it ended the way it did.

I couldn't let Vell kill him. I knew that's why he came to Houston. I had to walk away from Malik in order to let him live. It was the hardest thing I ever had to do, but I had to do it. Every step I took I could feel a knife slicing my heart. It hurt my soul the way he looked at me when I left with Vell. It was the only way to save his life was to sacrifice my happiness. If I would've stayed, Vell wouldn't have hesitated to off him. I couldn't have that on my heart.

I called Malik a few times since I've been back, and he won't take any of my calls to let me explain myself. I wanted him to hear me out. I wanted to explain myself. I don't want to be stupid or weak for Vell, because he embarrassed the fuck out of me. I know he's sorry, but I don't forgive that easy. My heart and trust aren't set up that way," I sighed.

"Look Leah I can't judge you at all. I'm not taking up for Vell because he's my brother. I've been in your shoes with Shon before. If you love Vell, be with him. Fuck what anybody else has to say. They're going to talk regardless. Let them talk. I want you to be happy even if it's not with him," she stated. Layla was real as fuck and I appreciate her for keeping it real, despite Vell being her brother. Shon was lucky to have her in his life. Malone and Layla were my biggest supporters through all this little bullshit we've been going through.

"In all my years of living, I've never listened to my heart. No matter what I've always done the opposite. I'm so scared to listen to my heart because my heart got me in trouble the last time. I don't like what being hurt feels like. It hurts so bad. Why does love, have to hurt?

When I found out about Vell and Mignon that shit hurt my soul. I would never smile up in a chicks face and fuck her man no matter how I felt about her." I cried. Ugh, and it's the tears and the pain that makes me say fuck Vell because I'm sick of doing this. I'm tired of these fuckin' tears. Why won't they fuckin' stop? It pisses me off.

"Awe Leah don't cry. I know it hurts and my heart hurts because he hurt you. Let that hurt go. Vell is the only one the can mend your broken heart because he damaged it. Hurt people hurt people and that's not healthy. The two of you done enough of that. Trust me, Vell is hurting too because he hurt you and you haven't taken him back. It's been six months. Yes, I'm counting. Sometimes I feel like I'm in the middle. Sphinx's having to tell me to stay out of it. I just want you two to be happy. Our family is so close. I miss seeing you and Vell on the love tip. I swear you make him better," she explained and laughed. I threw my throw pillows at her. "I'm just trying to set the mood Leah to give you a push," she laughed and threw the throw pillow back at me. I love our weekly girls' night where we can sit back and chill and talk and sip slow. We finished eating, and I had a lot of shit on my mind, Vell and Malik. I'm torn in between the two. I could never be with Malik because Vell wouldn't allow it.

Malone and Leah helped me clean up my kitchen and left. It was just me at home all alone in my thoughts. The only person that could sort them out is LaVell Baptiste. I guess it was time for us to have this talk that I've been avoiding. I don't know what the fuck we're doing. We haven't talked since Houston. Every time he tries to talk, I curve his ass. I didn't have anything to say because he said enough and done enough. I grabbed my phone off the coffee table. I sat back on the couch and threw my throw blanket over me. I tucked my feet underneath the pillows. I moved from my old spot. I had too because Vell was doing pop ups and he had me scared to go to sleep.

My heart and mind were fighting each other. I decided to listen to my heart for the second time in my life. I'm praying my heart doesn't lead me in the wrong direction. I toyed with my phone for a few a minute. I decided to go ahead and bite the bullet and call him. No matter how many times I deleted his number. I still knew it by heart. The call finally connected. The phone rung twice and I was just about to hang up until he answered.

"Yo," he yelled through the phone. I could tell he was in the trap.

"Are you busy?" I sighed.

"I'm never too busy for you Leah. Are you okay? Do I need to pull up?" he asked.

"No Vell, I'm good. I was just thinking about us," I sighed. A small smile appeared on my face. Vell was crazy as hell. I love him no matter how hard I try to fight it. I can't shake him. When he pulled up in Houston, I knew shit was real. I always wanted a man to love me this much.

"Oh yeah, I stay thinking about us. I'm ready to come home, Leah. I want to be at home with you. I miss holding you," he sighed and pleaded. Vell knew exactly what to say, but he needed to show me. He has been trying to show me.

"My heart still hurts Vell," I sniffled. I had to drop the phone to stop the tears from falling. I wasn't supposed to still be crying over him. I couldn't help it.

"Leah don't cry. I'm sorry let me love that hurt out of you? Can I make it right, please? Allow me to fix it? Allow me to fix us. All I'm asking is for another chance. I know I fucked up. I'm paying for that shit every day because I know you're not fucking with me. Leah, I can't say I was really dealt a bad hand. My mother did everything she could for us. I really don't remember much about my father, but he wasn't in the picture like a father should've been.

You saw first-hand what we went through. My mother was always there for us, but a woman can't teach a man how to be a man. My mother taught me what love is. She showed me how to love. I won't use my father as an excuse to why I did what I did. I was stupid as hell and too old to even be playing young nigga games because I'm a grown ass man.

I know right from wrong and I never wanted to hurt you, Leah. I love you and I love loving you. In this crazy world that we exist in you're the only thing that makes sense to me. We make sense. The moment you took your love away from me, my life has been fucked up. Yeah, I've been partying and bull shitting but it's no fun because I would rather be laid up under you. I'm paying for all the pain and bullshit I caused you. I've taken plenty of losses and I'm dealing with it, the best way I know how."

"I got to go Vell." I sniffled.

"Why Leah," he asked?

"Because I'm tired of crying Vell. I swear to God I am. The headaches are killing me."

"Open the door Leah and let me in, you can cry on me, baby? Since I'm the one who caused you so much pain?"

"How do you know where I live?"

"I know everything Leah. You don't know how many nights I've sat outside debating rather or not I wanted to run up in your spot and just hold you. Are you going to keep me out here all night in the cold or you're going to let me in?" He asked and pleaded. I unlocked the door and allowed Vell access to my home. He followed me inside. My nerves are a wreck. It's been months since we've been alone without fussing and fighting. Vell walked up behind me.

He wrapped his arms around my waist and ran his tongue up the crease of my neck. He sent chills through my body. I broke down crying again. Vell turned me around to face him. He removed a loose strand of hair from my face. He lifted me up and took a seat on the couch. He cupped my face and wiped my tears with his thumbs.

"Shh stop crying, Leah. Baby, I'm sorry. I swear I'm sorry for what I've done. I don't want you crying because of me. I hate your tears are because of me and some shit I've done. Can I love the hate out of your heart," he asked? My mind is telling me, no, but the heart is about to jump out my chest begging me to say yes.

"What would be different this time around Vell? Why should I say yes? Why should I trust you again?" I asked.

"I'm different Leah. Actions speak louder than words and I'm all about action. Let me show you. I want to earn your trust. I don't want you to give it to me, I want to work for it and work for you. I'm ready to put in work for you." He explained.

"Okay Vell. We can give us a shot again. I believe you and I want to see. The first time I feel that you're on some bullshit I'm gone. You will never see or hear from me again."

"Thank you. I swear to God I'm not going to fuck up. I got you Leah and I'm never letting you go. Where's your ring? I want you to put it back on your finger until I upgrade it? Grab your purse I want you to come back home." I grabbed my purse and Vell locked my door. How did he have a key to my spot? I better not regret this shit at all.

Chapter 19

Vell

Leah and I are finally back on good terms and I'm forever grateful and thankful for that. We still had a few issues that we needed to work out, but so far so good. Leah and I would've never broken up if it wasn't for Yona. She didn't know me and the worst thing she could've ever done was open her mouth to Leah about what the fuck I had going on. I'm man enough to admit that I needed to get caught to stop cheating and fucking with Mignon. All it took was one time. A bitch can't snitch on me without consequences. It's always action when it comes to me.

I stay in my lane and she should've stayed in hers but nah she had to swerve. It's a must I hit that bitch where it hurts. She knew I was a crazy nigga and didn't give a fuck. She's about to see how much I don't give a fuck. I could give two fucks about taking a female's life that doesn't mean me any good. I got a hit list and Yona is the first and only bitch on the list. I'm a nigga about my business and handling this shit today. She wouldn't live another day after fucking up my relationship because Shon didn't want her.

She couldn't compare to my sister. I don't even know why she was trying to fucking compete? There's no fuckin' comparison. I've been watching her for six months now. I've been waiting for the perfect time to handle her. Now was the time because she wouldn't expect me to get at her ass. She's been moving around care free knowing damn well she got a target on her back for snitching and hating on me. Its levels to this shit and she ain't on my level. She will be right after I catch her body.

"Vell, you're a crazy motherfucka. That's why I fuck' with you the long way. I'm going through the front door and you can bum rush the back door." I slapped hands with Zo and followed his move. My nigga was always on go. Yona lived in a house on the corner of Flat Shoals and Waldrop Road. This little chick that stayed two doors down from her grand momma fucked with my nigga Yayo, she gave us the drop. She said Yona just made it home, she just came from down there. I looked at the side of the house.

My nigga Gunz and One-way were dousing the outside of the house. We had this bitch surrounded. Nobody inside was leaving up out this bitch alive. I gave Zo the signal to kick that bitch in.

He fired a few shots and I could feel the house shake from the impact. My nigga Uno ran in right behind him to douse that bitch with gasoline. I jogged to the back of the house. I saw a little movement, fuck it. It's fuckin' go time, and anything moving was about to be still because I was killing it.

"It's a shame these motherfuckas got to die because Yona couldn't keep her mouth shut. Number one rule to these streets, never snitch on a nigga like me. I play for keeps out here. Any nigga or bitch that was in the business of coming between me and Leah had to go.

No face, no case. I'm not catching a case. Zo fired off a few shots. I could feel the house shake from the shot gun that nigga was toting. He was making a mess. I could smell death making its way to the kitchen. It was an older lady in the kitchen hiding behind the refrigerator.

She held her hands up. I hated to do it, but I had too. I had a black bandana doused in poison. I put it to her nose and she passed out instantly. I combed through the house looking for Yona. Zo and Uno laid every motherfuckin' body in this bitch down. The smell of death was seeping through the home. I kicked the bathroom door open and it was clear. I checked both bedrooms on the right and they were empty. It was one bedroom on the left, we heard a little movement. We stood outside for a minute. I placed my ear to the door to make sure I wasn't tripping. I tried to turn the doorknob, but it was locked. "Bingo," I mumbled. I kicked that bitch open.

"Bitch bring you ass out here," my OG Zo yelled. Yona didn't know ZO, that's why I wanted him to do it because she wouldn't recognize his voice. He opened the closet and that bitch was empty. I knew she couldn't escape out the window. My niggas were sitting in front of her house waiting to light her ass up if she tried to run. I flipped the bed over and Yona was hiding under the bed with the phone in her hand.

I snatched the phone out of her hand and ended the call. She called twelve, scary ass bitches. Anytime you're running your mouth you'll have to be prepared. I snatched my ski-mask off. I wanted this bitch to look me in the face. I had to do this shit quick because I knew them motherfuckas was on the way. The precinct is right down the street. It won't take too long for dispatch to send a squad car through here.

"What's going on Vell-," she cried and stuttered. Before she could even say my name good. I shoved my Glock 45 in her mouth. Tears were forming in the corners of her eyes. Why the fuck was she crying and stuttering? She wanted to do all this extra shit.

When she aired out all my fuckin' business there was no crying or fuckin' stuttering involved. I whispered in her ear where she could hear me. "Yona you're surprised to see me. Bitch you leaving this world today. I came to catch a body and I'm not leaving this motherfucka until I catch yours. You fucked up my life temporarily. I have to take yours permanently." This bitch could have another phone in here recording me. I don't trust this bitch.

"Come on OG let's clear it Yayo said the boys are on the way. The just busted a left on Waldrop." I let my Glock 45 rip. Yona was gone. One shot to the fuckin' head. Zo started dousing the house with gasoline. He dropped a match in Yona's room and a fire started instantly. This motherfucking was blazing.

We jogged through the house quickly pouring gasoline and throwing matches. Yona's grandmother had a basement in her house. It had a side door, and that was our exit. I doused the basement with gasoline and it caught on fire instantly. We took off instantly toward the woods in the back. I heard the sirens closing in on us. Our car was parked two streets over.

Yayo sent me a text and said the police just pulled up and the fire truck was right behind them. It looks like they can hold off on going inside. The gasoline was laced with bleach and ammonia.

"You're a wild ass nigga Vell. I feel you though I would've done the same shit if a bitch came between Alexis and me. I'm glad you and Leah worked it out. She's a good chick and she deserves the world for putting up with your ass." He chuckled. I'm glad Leah and I finally worked it out too.

I was missing her like crazy. I still want to marry her soon. Alonzo and I pulled off in traffic. I had to stop by the funeral home and get rid of these clothes. Then take this car to the chop shop just in case it's on camera. You could never be too sure. Alonzo and I finished chopping it up and went our separate ways. I was ready to make it back home to my baby. I couldn't let Yona live another day after she did what she did to us.

I finally made it to the house. Leah moved back into the house that we once shared. I was doing 90 mph just to make it back home to her. As soon as I opened the door, she was in the kitchen cooking in her bra and panties. The food smelled good too, but the only thing I wanted to eat was her, that's all she's allowing me to do. I walked up behind her and wrapped my arms around her stomach. I inhaled her scent because she smelled so good.

I ran my tongue up the side of her neck and placed a few bites on her neck marking my territory. She smelled so good. I could tell she just got out of the shower. I could smell her body wash dripping from her pores. Her hair was still wet and pulled up in a loose ponytail. Leah was thick as fuck. She was shaped like a twenty-ounce coke cola bottle. Her body was covered in tattoos. Her skin was the color of Reese's peanut butter cup and she always wore the sexiest lingerie. Her breasts were sitting up high, begging to be freed from the bra that was suffocating them.

Her ass was swallowing that thong. I grab a hand full of her ass. I had to adjust my dick because it's been a minute since I've murdered that pussy. I was still in the doghouse. I wasn't complaining if she was at home with me and we were together.

"Stop Vell," she squirmed and moaned. She was trying to break free from my embrace but that wasn't happening. I missed the fuck out of Leah.

I was on a mission. I lifted Leah up and sat her on the counter top. I slid my hands in her panties. She was already wet for a nigga. I slid the thong down her thick thighs and started to finger fuck Leah wet. I began to speed up the pace.

I could tell she was about to cum, her juices were running down the counter. I ran my tongue in the puddle, slurping all that shit up.

I removed my fingers and threw her legs over my shoulder. I devoured the pussy. She was running from me. I could tell she was about to cum. I felt her body jerk twice.

She came all on my face. I didn't give a fuck; a nigga missed this shit. Leah has been teasing the fuck out of me for a minute. We've been back together for two months and she still hasn't let me touch her. She's been giving me blue balls. I can't wait to take a shower. I'm patient. I swear to God I am. I wanted to rape her ass many nights. In the middle of the night, I wake up to workout. I'm not even tripping off that.

"Leah I'm about to take a shower, I'll be back in a minute." Leah grabbed my shirt. I looked over my shoulders to see what she wanted.

"Vell, what's wrong?" she sighed. Leah sounded sad. I haven't done shit.

"Come here Leah, nothing's wrong." She did as she was told. Leah folded her arms across her chest. She poked her lips out looking at me. I cupped her chin forcing her to look at me. "What's wrong baby talk to me, what I do?"

"I thought you were mad at me because we haven't had sex yet," she sighed and put her head down. I cupped her chin forcing her to look at me again. I could never be mad at Leah. I love her too much.

"I want you Leah and only you. Ain't shit a bitch can do for me out here. It took me losing you for six months to realize that. I ain't pressed for the pussy. Do I want it? Hell yeah, I do. I can't wait to dive in and murder it, but I know we'll cross that line when we get there."

Leah

Vell and I have been back together for two months now. So far everything has been going well and I can't complain. He brought me a suite. So, I've been picking out a few pieces to setup my boutique. I've been thinking of a name for weeks. Malone and I finally came up with one. **Pieces of Lea'.** We haven't had sex yet. I wasn't ready, but tonight I wanted to take it there. I cooked a nice dinner for us. I wanted it to be a surprise. Vell has been real patient with me. Every night he holds me and whispers sweet nothings in my ears. His dick pokes me in my ass. Something was different with Vell tonight.

Since we've been together, he never comes home and went straight to the shower. Something was up with that. I hope he wasn't fucking somebody else because I wasn't giving him any pussy. I trusted Vell. I don't think he's on any bullshit. I cut the stove off because our dinner was already finished. I walked upstairs to our room. I could tell he hasn't been in the shower that long because the window wasn't foggy. I stripped naked and decided to join him. Vell was in the shower with his eye's clothes stroking his dick. I tapped him on his shoulder and he turned around and looked at me. I ran my tongue across my bottom lip.

"Can I help you with that?" I asked. Vell looked at me as if he was unsure if he wanted to answer.

"Are you sure Leah. I'm not trying to pressure you if you're not ready?"

"I'm ready." I pushed Vell up against the base of the shower and I squatted in front of him. I took his dick into my mouth and I made sure my mouth was extra wet. I coughed up a glob of spit to make sure the spit covered Vell's dick. I took him in my mouth inch by inch. Spit was running down the side of my mouth. Vell grabbed my hair with so much force and started fuckin' my mouth. I grabbed his legs for support and swallowed him whole. I could feel his dick touch the back of my throat. I started to gag a little bit. I spit on his dick and started humming. I could tell Vell was about to cum. I could taste the pre-cum.

"I'm about to cum Leah." He grunted and moaned. I applied pressure and sucked a little harder. Vell busted all down my throat and I drained his ass.

I opened my mouth and tasted the shower water. I gargled a little bit and spit the water out. I attempted to walk out the shower and Vell grabbed me from me behind. I looked over my shoulder and gave him a nasty little smirk. I grabbed his hand and led him to the bedroom. I crawled in the bed, and as soon as my head reached the headboard, I motioned with my hand for him to come join me. Vell was looking at me and smiling.

He knew it was about to go down. I haven't had sex in seven months. It was way overdue for some. Vell grabbed the towel off the bed and he finished drying off. He motioned with his hand for me to come to him. I crawled to him. He picked me up and I wrapped my legs around his waist. He wrapped his hands around my waist, holding me in place. My breasts were touching his chest. Our foreheads were touching each other. He grabbed my face roughly, stroked my cheek, and cupped my chin. I gazed up at him. I wanted him, and the suspense was killing me. He leaned forward and gave me a kiss.

"I love you Leah, I don't want to fuck you. I want to make love to you. Can I have my way with you," he asked. I nodded my head yes. "I don't understand body language. I want to hear it." He explained. Since when doesn't he read body language?

"I love you to Vell. I want you to make love to me. What are you waiting on?" I asked. I wrapped my arms around his neck. Vell bit my bottom lip. He was staring me in my eyes. He had me uncomfortable. I didn't know what to expect.

"I've suffered a lot of consequences and I've learned a lot of lessons. I thank God for this blessing. I appreciate and value you. If loving, you were a crime I wouldn't give a fuck about doing the time. I took plenty of risks I'll admit. Thank you for giving me another chance. You belong to me and I belong to you. Remember that. I want forever with you. I don't ever want to beef or be at odds with you. I know we're starting over fresh, but baby I can't wait to marry you. I know repairing your heart takes time and if it ever stops beating, I swear to God I'll give you mine. I don't ever want you to leave me again. You're the air I breathe. Leah, will you marry me?" He asked. His proposal was so sweet. I couldn't believe he still wanted to marry little old me. I couldn't stop the tears from falling.

"Yes Vell, I'll marry you!" I yelled. Vell tossed me on the bed. He reached in the nightstand and opened a box that was rose gold, and he pulled out a new ring. I swear to God it was the biggest one I had ever seen. It had to be at least 18 karats. It was stacked with three different shapes of rings. The different shapes of diamonds were blinding me. It was different, and I loved it. He slid it on my finger and I couldn't stop looking at it. Vell climbed on top me. I opened my legs giving Vell easy access. I tilted my head back trying to get a good look at him. It didn't take him long to get comfortable inside of me. He started sucking my breasts and I started grinding a little bit on him. Vell was hung and it's been a while since we felt each other.

"Don't move Leah, be still. I got you." I had to get used to his size again. He threw my legs over his waist. I scooted back a little bit. He pulled his dick out and started playing with my pussy getting it extra wet. Then he shoved his dick back inside of me. My body tensed up easily. I was tight damn near a virgin. Tears formed in the corner of my eyes. I blinked twice so they wouldn't run down my face.

"Let them fall, Leah, it's all good. I'm about to make you feel really good." He started pounding my pussy, long deep, and hard. His dick felt so good. I wanted to match his rhythm stroke for stroke, but I couldn't. I was in bliss. I was getting high off this shit. Vell was my drug of choice and right now I was overdosing on love. I was addicted to his touch and fiending for a nut. I said a quick prayer hoping he doesn't ease up. Any other time I would've ridden this big motherfucka as my life depended on it, but not today because Vell was having his way with me. It's been a long time coming and I wouldn't have it any other way. This is the beginning of something new.

"Can I bury my seeds, Leah?" He asked through moans and grunts. I had to look at Vell to make sure I was hearing him correctly. I wanted a son for the longest. If Vell was ready to have kids, then it means he's leaving the game. I told him I wasn't having any babies if he was still in the streets.

"Are you leaving the streets Vell. I'm not raising a child alone," I moaned.

"Yes, I'm leaving them. I've been trying to do it for a minute now. Since I have you back, I'm ready to start my family. I got plans to do a lot of legit shit. I'm ready to start a family."

"Yes, you can bury your seeds." Vell and I went at it for hours until the sun came up. We didn't even get the chance to eat dinner. We trashed the food and made breakfast.

Chapter 20

Layla

*S*hon I'm leaving and finding me and Shalani a place to live." I sighed. I'm tired. I know Shon is working but he doesn't make enough time for us. I'm not doing this with him. I refuse to continue to keep living like this. It's killing me mentally. I expected so much more from him and I'm tired of all the empty promises. Sometimes things don't work out and I'm okay with that.

"Come on Layla why are you tripping? You know my daughter isn't leaving this house. Neither is her mother," he argued. I ignored Shon. I meant what the fuck I said. I grabbed Shalani's diaper bag off the sofa and headed to the kitchen to grab the milk that I pumped earlier. Shon grabbed my hand trying to stop me from leaving. I stopped in my tracks refusing to turn around and look at him.

"Layla where are you going?" Why would he ask a question that he already knew the answer too? I swear this is one of the hardest things I ever had to do in my life, but I *had to do it. I had to stand for something because I was tired of falling for anything. I showed Shon one time and I'll show him again.*

"Sphinx and Malone's." I sighed. I could never tell Shon where I was really going.

"Don't do that Layla, please. Let me take the two of you out to lunch and I'll treat you to a massage later."

"Okay, Shon."

I couldn't stop replaying the conversation that Shon and I had earlier. It's 8:00 p.m. and he still hasn't made it home yet. He's taking my kindness for my weakness. He thinks that I won't leave, and I will.

I love Shon Adams with all my heart. I always have, and I always will. I've been patient with Shon for a very long time. I don't have any more patience. To be honest I've been patient with him my whole life. I refuse to continue to roll with the punches. The moment Shon and I laid eyes on each other again. I knew it would land us right here. Every time I look at our daughter, she's a reflection of the love that we share. I wrote Shon a nice letter. I wasn't playing with him.

I'm a grown ass woman and I refuse to shack with any man that's not my husband. Shon isn't excluded. Where in the fuck do, they do that at? I hope Shon didn't think I was the same woman that I was ten years ago? More of the reason why Cree knew he had to put a ring on it. I refuse to tolerate what Cree or Shon was offering. I had no problems with getting the fuck on. I went through a lot with Shon and I refuse to do this shit again. I'm not doing it. It feels like history is repeating itself.

It goes against everything that I believe in. I'm not going against shit I believe in this time around. I hate to separate our family, but it is what it is. Shon must come correct until he does that, he can be by himself. I sat the ring on the dresser. I wrote Shon a nice letter. I'm going to stay at my mother's house with my daughter.

I finally made it to my mother's house. Shalani was starting to get fussy. Probably because she was looking for her father. I hate to take her away from Shon, but I had to stand for something. He was taking me for granted. I was way past tired of it. I grabbed her out of her car seat and carried her into the house. My phone started ringing and it was Shon. I looked at the clock and it was after 10:00 p.m. which means he just got home. I wasn't answering right now. I had to get my daughter situated. I finally got Shalani situated. I gave her a hot bath and it was time to breast feed her and hopefully she'll go to bed and let me get a good night's sleep. I grabbed my phone off the charger and decided to call Shon back. He answered on the first ring.

"Yo Layla, what the fuck are you trying to prove? Bring your ass home and bring my daughter back home too. Better yet where the fuck are you so I can pull up." He argued and yelled through the phone. I removed the phone from my ear. Shon was talking reckless and loudly. I don't know who Shon thought he was talking too, but I wasn't the one. Shon can continue to be mad because I'm not coming back home. It's his fault. When a woman is fed up, it's nothing you can do about it. He wanted me to roll with the punches, it's time for him to roll with my punches.

"Shon lower your voice. I called you back and I was very calm. If you want to go there, we fuckin' can. Don't talk to me like I'm an average bitch on the street because I'm not. I'm not coming back home. Respect me and what the fuck I'm doing. I refuse to continue to shack up with you. I'm not comfortable doing it and I refuse to continue to be uncomfortable. I'll bring your daughter home tomorrow to see you." I argued. Shon can't talk to me any kind of way because he's upset. It's not happening.

"Layla you ain't shacking up with me. Why aren't you comfortable? I give you everything you want and need. When do you want to get married? I told you to plan our wedding months ago and I'll be there. Bring my baby home. I want her mother at home too." He argued. I wasn't hearing anything Shon was saying. If he wanted to get married, then we should be planning a wedding, not just me.

"Good night Shon, I'll see you tomorrow. Step up or I'm stepping the fuck away. I swear to God I am. I'm not making any threats. It's a promise." I said what I had to say, and I hung up. Shon was selfish as fuck and he can continue to be by himself. I'm not putting up with his shit. I didn't move back here to deal with this. I could've stayed in Miami. I didn't ask to come here, he brought me back. Plan a wedding? I can't believe him. Clearly, I'm the only one in this relationship.

What happened to us planning a wedding? Nah, Shon, I'm good. I 'm not begging any nigga to marry me no matter how much I love him. I'm good and this the reason why I left. I'm too old to be his girlfriend. I'm never going to be anybody's baby momma forever. Miss me with that bullshit. He started calling my phone back.

"What Shon Adams?" I argued. I had so much base in my voice as if he could see me.

"I'm on my way, Layla Adams." He chuckled. This man really thinks I'm playing with him. If he thinks he can track my location, he has life fucked up.

"It's Baptiste until the death of me. You don't have any papers on me. It's plenty of men out here. I guess it's time for me to put this pussy back on the market. I knew it wouldn't work out. You can stay where you are Shon. Have a nice life I'm trying to get used to sleeping by myself." I sighed and hung up. I cut my phone off. I wasn't about to keep going back and forth with Shon. We're grown as fuck. He can find another bitch to play with because I don't want to play the games he's trying to play.

Shon

Dear Shon

I can't believe I'm even writing you this letter. We shouldn't have even come to this. I swore we were way past this stage. The last time I left you, I didn't even write a letter, but since there's a child involved, I'll have to move a little different. I'm grown and more mature now. I'm leaving you because I'm tired of you taking me for granted. You've tried me for the last fuckin' time. We've been apart years and you still don't get it. You probably never will. Guess what? It's my fault for believing that you would change. I don't even want to figure this shit out anymore. My life doesn't revolve around you. Something must give. I don't have anything else to give. I'm leaving you and I'm taking Shalani with me. I won't keep her from you, but I will keep myself away from you.

Don't come looking for me, unless you're ready to take the next step. I can't believe I'm giving you an ultimatum. Respect my wishes and my space. Entertain a bitch in my absence and I'm killing you and her, that's a fuckin' promise. Please don't test my fuckin' gangsta.

Love Layla

L ayla got me fucked up. It ain't no breaking or sleeping in different houses when you have my daughter. We're in a relationship and she's trying to fuckin' walk out on me. Layla and I shared locations on our iPhone. She had the nerve to write me a letter. I tore that shit up. I grabbed my phone to see where Layla was with my daughter. Layla cut her location off. She got me fucked up. I called Malone to see if she knew where Layla was hiding. She answered on the first ring.

"What Shon I'm not telling you where Layla is. If you would've brought your ass home sooner you would've been able to stop her," she argued and spewed. I had to look at the phone to make sure I wasn't tripping.

"Malone, am I your brother? Damn, you're doing it like that now?" I asked. She's supposed to be team me no matter what. I'm not with the games that Layla and Malone are playing. She has my daughter and I need to know her whereabouts.

"Shon, Layla is my sister. I'm a woman before anything. It's important that black woman stick together no matter what. I'm riding with her right or wrong. Look,

Shon, do what the fuck you need to do, to make her happy. Y'all have been together forever. I want her to be your wife. She's my sister n law regardless because her brother is my husband.

Layla isn't playing with your ass. She's tired and fed up. She doesn't care how much money you have or what you do for her. She has her own bag. I'll call my wedding planner to get the ball rolling because SHON you are about to miss the fuckin' boat. Y'all have history and an amazing chemistry. Don't let your pride make you lose your family. You're fuckin' up big time. Time waits for no man. Why should you be excluded? You did a whole fuckin' lot to get to this point," she argued stated.

"I hear you Malone and I'm listening. I'm going to do better I swear to God I am. I need Layla to be patient with a nigga Malone. Everything we went through and everything I've taken her through wasn't in vain. I'm not trying to rush shit. She's going to be my wife regardless. I'm not about to play these games with her. She won't win fuckin' with a nigga like me. She thought it was easy leaving me the last time. I wish she would try that shit again. It's not going down like that. Ain't nobody coming in between that. She already knows how I'm coming every fuckin' time." I argued. "She saw what the fuck happened to Cree."

"I hear you Shon, handle your business. You have a beautiful family. Layla deserves the world." Malone and I finished wrapping it up with each other. Layla wanted a little space to prove her point. She knows there's no such thing as space when it comes to us. I'll find her. I love the fuck out of Layla and my daughter. She knows that. Layla wanted more from me and I don't mind giving her that. I'm not trying to rush shit. She got to be patient. I'm ready to get married.

She heard what the fuck I said, she can plan our wedding if she's ready. She hasn't even attempted to plan our wedding. I'm marrying her when I feel the time is right for us. I should've been done it, but it's a lot of shit going on out here in these streets. Things are getting back to normal slowly but surely. A nigga ain't use to laying by himself at night. I was tired. I needed to lay down. Layla is stressing me the fuck out. I threw the pillow over my head and went to sleep.

"Damn baby right there. Cree, it feels so good. I missed this dick baby. I love the way you fuck me and make my body feel," she moaned. She was really fuckin' this nigga while my daughter was asleep lying in her basinet. *I'm going to kill her motherfuckin' ass.*

"Layla this pussy still gets super wet for a nigga. I love the way your juices coat my dick. You're my Milk Marie, this pussy so pretty," he moaned. *I know I'm not tripping. I killed this nigga. If she lied about him being dead, I'm going to kill her fuckin' ass.* My phone rung waking me up from this horrible dream I was having.

I jumped up quick and grabbed my AK-47 out the closet. Layla is about to die today. My phone rang again, and it was my mother. I answered my phone to see what my mother wanted.

"Yeah ma what's up?" I yelled. I ain't got time for her shit. I need a location on Layla.

"Open the fuckin' door nigga, I've been out here for over an hour. My trap got hit. I'm missing three fuckin' bricks. I did the count and I didn't sign off on that shit. I need you to handle it or else I'm laying every motherfuckin' body in that bitch down Shon. A motherfucka can't steal from me and live to tell about it. Don't fuck with my family and my bread and we won't have any problems." She argued. I buzzed my mother in and she's been talking shit ever since she hit the slab.

"I'll handle it. Do you know where Layla is staying with my daughter?" I asked. I grabbed the desert eagle from the living room closet. Layla and that nigga both are about to die. I might have been dreaming, but that shit seemed real as fuck. I put that shit on Twin if she's out giving my pussy away and my daughter's lying next to her. I'm killing her ass and I'll be ready for Sphinx and Vell. She left so she could go and fuck another nigga. She knows I don't play that shit.

"Shon what the fuck is wrong with you and where are you going this time of night? I just left the house, you can handle that shit in the morning," she argued. My mother knew I was on one. The only way I'll calm down is when I find Layla and my daughter.

"I got a lot of shit on my mind. I'll handle the trap right now. I got to run down on Layla. I just had a dream she was fucking another nigga ma. I swear to God I'm gone kill her. I know you know, where she's at ma. Tell me or

I'm going to call AT&T and tell them to give me her location." I argued. I ain't never had a dream about Layla fuckin' another nigga.

"Shon you need to chill out. You know Layla would never do that. It doesn't feel good does it, laying by yourself at night? Get your shit together Shon, before she makes you replaceable. Layla's a bad bitch. I got to give it to her. She can have any man she wants too, but she chose you. She's at Shaolin's and don't tell her I fuckin' told you. I mean that shit.

It's 2018 women aren't waiting on niggas to get their shit together. Especially if they have theirs together. Give me one reason why she should wait on you? Women aren't waiting for men to marry them, they'll find a man that's ready. It's plenty of them out here. You disrupted Layla's life for what? You couldn't stand to see another man with something you had. Make an honest woman out of her or move the fuck on. Shon you don't want to watch the next nigga do it. I'm keeping that shit 95 with you, Shon. I'm tired of telling you. I'm your mother, but I'm a woman before anything. You let her get away once being stupid. Don't let her get away twice, she won't give two fucks about your threats. Another man will be glad to be Shalani's stepfather." She argued and explained.

"Over my dead fuckin' body momma. That shit ain't happening. I hear you, momma, good looking out. I know what I need to do." Damn everybody's on me hard as fuck about Layla and me.

I pulled up to Shaolin's house. I already knew the code to her house. Vell, Sphinx, and I take turns coming over here to check shit out. I combed my way through Shaolin's looking for Layla. I had my Desert Eagle cocked and ready. She was upstairs in the guest bedroom.

My daughter was lying right next to her. I pulled the covers back and Layla was butt ass naked. I pried her legs open to see if she's been fuckin' off on me. Layla woke up instantly panicking. What the fuck was she so jumpy for?

"Shon what the fuck are you doing?" she argued. Layla was a little too loud and about to wake my daughter up.

"It's my pussy, Layla, what the fuck you mean what am I doing? I'm asking the questions not you. You didn't want me to come over here because you were laid up over here fuckin' another nigga? Get your ass up and put some clothes on. Let's go because this ain't fuckin' home." I argued. I grabbed Layla's hand and put her ring back on her finger. I woke my daughter up, and she started cooing. "Daddy missed you. Mommy's trying to keep daddy's princess away from him."

"Shon don't start that shit. How dare you come in here and accuse me of cheating on you because I left our house. I ain't never cheated on you and I should've. I'm a grown ass woman and I don't have to cheat on you. I'll just leave your ass and you know that from experience. We don't have to even throw jabs at each other. You know what it is with me. Did you find what you were looking for because the door is that way," she argued. Layla just didn't know she had me ready to fuck her being so feisty. She was turning a nigga on and didn't even know it.

"Layla I'm not leaving this house without you and my daughter. Whatever issues we have we can work that out at home." I argued.

"Shon, you don't get it do you? I refuse to shack with you again. I'm not fucking doing it anymore. We can be together, but we don't have to live together unless we're married. I mean that shit. I'm not pressuring, you to marry me and I'll never make you do nothing that you don't want to do. Let me stay here," she argued.

"Layla, come here this ain't even us. I love you Layla, on some real shit. I do want to marry you. I want you to be my wife. I want my family. Bear with me please Layla, that's all I'm asking. Come here please." I asked and begged.   ·

"Okay, Shon." She sighed. Layla walked over to me. I pulled her into my lap. I started massaging her shoulders to relax her a little bit. She was very tense. I rested my chin on the nape of her neck. Home would always be with Layla and she knows that. We were both in deep thought. I had some shit I wanted say.

"Layla, you know I love you right?" I asked. It's important that she knows that.

"I'm listening Shon, say what you need to say." She argued and sassed. I wrapped my arms around her waist.

"I love you, Layla, never doubt that. Don't count me out. Please don't because I'm going to come through.

You can count on me. Since we've been back together things have been different. We're different. In this crazy world, you're the only thing that makes sense. I don't want you to be my girlfriend either, the moment we got back together. I knew I had to make you my wife. It's only right. I want my forever with you. Marrying you has always been the plan. I'm a grown ass man. I know what I want this time around. It's you and only you. Please don't get it confused.

I want you to carry my last name. We've come a long way. I love waking up to you and my daughter every morning. We're raising our daughter in a two-parent household. Nothing or no one will change that. Not even you. The two of you are the high lights of my life. When I'm in these streets getting to this money, making it back home to you and her is a priority. I don't ask for much Layla. I'm asking you to be patient with me? I promise you everything will fall in place. I don't make promises that I can't keep. Marrying you isn't a promise, it's our reality. It's going to happen because I'm going to make it happen. I made you a promise that'll I stay true to you. You're special to me and I got something special planned for you. Do you trust me, Layla?"

"I trust you Shon and I hear you."

"Are you listening?"

"Yes, I'm listening. Why should I wait? Why should I believe you? We've been here before. The only difference now is that we have a child involved. I've been patient but I'm not going to continue to wait forever. I won't do it. I'll walk away Shon."

"Baby my word is all I have. I just want to love, cuff and cherish you. These past few months it's been a lot going on and you know that. Our life is finally falling in place. We have a history that can never be erased. I won't let you take that from me. Have faith in me, have faith in us. I believe in us. Trust the process. I was patient with you Layla when I was trying to win you back. Good things come to those who wait. I just want to make you happy. I took you for granted years ago, but I'll never do that again. If I didn't want to marry you. I would've never asked you. Are you happy despite everything that we've been through? Am I doing a good job?"

"Good night Shon. I'm not going back and forth with you. I'm tired and I'm sleepy. I just want to be left alone. I'll be patient with you outside of our home. You can leave now," she argued.

"I'm not leaving Layla I want you to come home. Why can't we work past our issues at home?"

"Good bye Shon. I'm tired. I don't want to talk about it anymore. I'll be patient as long as you respect my wishes." Layla tried to raise up from me and walk away. I wouldn't let her.

"I'm tired too. Can I lay with you? Can I hold you?"

"Can you?" I picked Layla up and laid her on my chest. Layla was crying silently. My chest was soaked. I swear she was breaking me down. I know her tears were because of me. I had a lot of shit on my mind. I wasn't about to lose Layla or my family. I had to get my shit together. I cupped her chin forcing her to look at me. I wiped her tears with my index fingers. I placed a kiss on her lips.

"Layla stop crying, please. I'm not trying to upset you. I If I hurt your feelings, I'm sorry. You got my heart. I want to make things right between us. I got you. I got us. I just want you to be happy."

"I want to be happy too. I promised myself I wouldn't do this with you. I haven't cried over you in years. Loving you hurts Shon and it shouldn't. It hurts so bad because I feel like you're playing with me. Why do you want to keep doing this to me? I've been questioning myself for the longest. Was this shit worth it?

I wouldn't trade my daughter for anything in this world, but I refuse to lose myself behind you. I'll trade my tears and my feelings any day because I don't want to endure the pain that comes with loving you," she cried.

"Come on Layla why are you trying to hurt my feelings? I'll never let you lose yourself behind me. I swear to God I'm not playing with you. Since we've been together it's been all about you. I don't want my love to hurt, that's some painful as shit you putting out there. I want this to work. Our relationship hasn't been perfect Layla. I'm not the man I used to be. Stop comparing our future to our past this shit will never last?

I thought we were starting over? You've never even given me a fair chance if you are basing our relationship on our past. I'm trying Layla damn, but you got to give me a fair chance. I'm not asking you to forget about what happened or forgive. Damn Layla, I thought we were building something new? You got to let that shit go. Do you love me, Layla, because right now I'm not so sure?" I argued.

"I have forgiven you, Shon, it just seems like history is repeating itself. You've promised me a lot and never came through. Before I let myself get hurt, I'll walk away from you." She cried.

"I'm not in this to hurt you. I don't want to hurt you. Baby, I need you. I love you and I'm not trying to live my life without you. Layla, I know what I'll have to do to make things right with you. I got you and I need you to have faith in us. I'm not an emotional ass nigga but damn you got me shedding a few tears myself because I'm hurting you. I'm lost without you." I explained. Layla drifted off to sleep. I couldn't even sleep. It's time for me to get my shit together. I love Layla and I got plans to hold her down until eternity.

Layla

"Who dropped the fuckin' bomb on me? I can't believe Shon done all that shit. It was so emotional. I was in my feelings and he was in his. I haven't cried over Shon in a long time. I hate crying. My face is all ugly and shit. I swore I woke up with a headache. I stood my ground and I didn't leave. I had so much on my chest and he just got the wrath of it" I sighed. I couldn't wait until Shon left so, I could call Malone and Leah. I had to feel them in on my night. I was sleeping peacefully until he came and showed his ass.

"It wasn't me Layla, I gave him the business. It was probably my momma." She stated. It probably was her. I'm not even surprised. She's riding with me right or wrong, but Shon can't do any harm in her eyes. I understand where Shon was coming from, but he wasn't put in a fucked-up situation, I was. He was content. He was living his life fuckin' different hoes and I was at home playing house. I know he's not doing that because he's always at home. I don't want to play house with him.

"It probably was. She always siding with him no matter what. I was caught off guard because he pried my legs open and started smelling my pussy. He thought I was really over here fucking a different nigga," I laughed. Shon is crazy. I knew he lost his fucking mind. I'm not that woman.

"Layla, I don't want to hear about Shon smelling your pussy to see if it's been fucked or not." Malone and Leah were both laughing. I can't stand they petty ass'. Every time Vell or Sphinx is on some good bull shit I'm the first motherfucka they call. I miss my bitches Tati and Trecie, they'll never judge me. They're always willing to hear me, but these bitches here.

"Fuck y'all I don't want to hear shit about my brothers and how good they slang dick. Since you two are doing it like that." I laughed. I can't stand them, they make me sick.

"I didn't even say anything Layla come on now." I had to go because Shalani was getting fussy. She missed her father. I'm going home tonight too. It took her forever to go to sleep last night.

Chapter-21

♥

Shon

"I swear to God Layla is going to be the death of me. She acts like she's trying to kill me. I'm not ready to die yet. I feel like shit. I had no clue she was feeling like this. I got to do what's right and step the fuck up. I want to be in my daughter's life. I don't want to co-parent with Layla. It's only right. She deserves more than that. My mother and father both raised me until a pussy ass nigga took him away from me. I respect my OG because she never let another man replace our father up until recently.

I plan on making her, my wife. It's been a lot of shit going on these pasts few months. I'm not an emotional ass nigga but Layla had me tearing the fuck up last night. I don't want to be the cause of her pain. I want to be the key to her happiness. I thought I was doing a good job, but I guess not. I'm fuckin up big time Dino.

My head ain't right. I can't even focus on the trap. I keep thinking about our last conversation. What if I never see her again? What if she fucks around and up and leaves me like last time? I keep checking the cameras at home every five minutes and she still hasn't come home yet. Layla was standing her ground and I couldn't do anything but respect that even if it's killing me. She deserves to be happy but I'm the only one that could give her that."

"I feel where you're coming from Shon. If you feel like that you need to make some shit happen. You surprised the fuck out of me in Miami. I just knew I would've been getting fit for a tux already. Let me keep it ninety-five with you. I've been there and done that. You know what the fuck I've been through. I love Tory and my daughters. I wouldn't trade them for anything in this world. I love being a family man. I had to get my shit together because she was going to fuck around and leave me.

I've fucked a lot of women and none of them can compare to her. Tory was with me when I didn't have shit. She was with me when I was wearing all your clothes. Shit, she was with me when my momma sold all our food stamps for dope. Her grandmother fed me every night and never judged me. When my momma wouldn't pay our light bill. I would sneak in Tory's room at night and sleep until Leilani found out how I was living, and she took me in. She ain't never asked me for shit but loyalty and respect. Tory knew I was out here being a dog ass nigga.

I thank God every day that she never left me or gave up on me. I wasn't worthy of her love. I took her for granted because I was young and dumb. I knew better because when I didn't have it, them bitches wasn't even thinking about me. The moment I got the bag, I switched up on Tory. Our money was just starting to pile up Shon. We were making about $20,000.00 a week. Shit, back then that was a blessing because I was a broke nigga. We were in South Dekalb Mall and The Candler Road Flee Market stunting. Yeah, I was breaking Tory off, but she didn't even want my money.

When a woman's fed up it ain't shit you can do about it. I almost lost it all when Keosha was running around saying she was pregnant by me. If Tory would've left Shon, I would've killed myself. Tory was done with my ass. I prayed every night Keosha son wasn't mine because if he was Tory was as good as gone. God came through for me. Some shit ain't worth loosing. I didn't want to lose her. I had to get my shit together.

You got a second chance with Layla. Don't fuck that up." He explained. Dino was my nigga, we've been down since the sand box. I trust him with my life. He will never steer me wrong. We finished chopping it up. I had a few runs to make and then I was heading home. I hope Layla finds her way home. It was time to give Layla my last name.

Layla

I had a little free time because Leilani wanted to keep Shalani for a few hours. I decided to go and get my nails and feet done. I needed my brows cleaned up also. I wanted to do a little Christmas shopping before I had to pick up Shalani. Leilani refused to let Shalani come with me. She was a little too young to be in the mall. I didn't want her to be exposed to germs. I had a lot of things on my mind and I had to get out of the house. It's crazy because I wanted to take a few Christmas pictures at the house with Shon and Shalani, but I don't know if that'll be happening because we're not in a good space.

I needed to swing by the house to get a few things while Shon wasn't at home. I rode past the Trap earlier and Shon and Dino's cars were parked out front, so I knew he wouldn't be home yet. I don't know how I feel after our conversation last night. I couldn't really talk to Malone and Leah about it. In all my years of living, I don't think I ever saw Shon cry. Something must give because we're both hurting. Hurt people hurt people. I said a lot of things that I shouldn't have, and I regret it. I really do. I was supposed to bring Shalani by the house to see him today, but I couldn't after what happened last night. I couldn't face him. Tears formed in my eyes just thinking about it. I grabbed a Kleenex from my arm rest and dabbed my eyes.

I finally made it home, but I was caught off guard because Shon was home and it was another car behind his. I didn't recognize the car and it wasn't any of our family members. We don't have company at our house unless it's family. I swear to God if Shon has another bitch in our home, we share I'm killing him and her. He got me so fucked up. It's funny because he hasn't called or texted me since he left this morning. He wanted me to leave so he could be disrespectful and cheat. I got something for his ass. Long live Shon. I always kept at least two guns in the car, you never know when you may need them. I pulled out my Glock 40 with my extended clip. I hate I had these open toed booties on, but I don't give a fuck. I'm about to see what's up. I loaded my gun and I made sure I had one in the chamber.

I couldn't use the garage because he would hear me. I wanted to catch his ass. I swear this feels like Deja Vu. Thank God our house was keyless. I went in through the back door. I entered the code on the keypad and crept in through the kitchen when I heard some noises. It wasn't a female but a male. I made my way out the kitchen because I wanted to hear what was going on.

"Aye Shon set that motherfuckin shit out. I know you left the Trap and didn't drop the count off. I followed you home. OG or should I call you pussy? That bitch got your mind gone you're not even paying attention to your surroundings," he argued and yelled. My heart started beating fast. Shon was being robbed and it's all my fault. I can't fuckin' lose him. I took my shoes off. I ran to the basement and got the 12 gauge. A motherfucka ain't leaving this bitch without dying. You can't violate my home or take anything that we've worked hard for. I maybe a lot of things, but a pussy or weak ass bitch ain't one of them. I've stood in the paint with Shon for years. I made it back upstairs to the living room. I sent Shon a text.

Mr. Adams - Life Until I Die, I Got Your Front and Back

I checked my phone and he read the text. All I could hear was a room being ransacked.

"Where's the safe and the fuckin' jewelry? You better get to talking before I start shooting. I'll get a lot of rank for taking out the plug," he argued and laughed. Typical young nigga shit. Over my fuckin' dead body. I've heard enough. I took the steps to our room two at a time. I made sure my steps couldn't be heard as I made it to the top. The 12 gauge was so heavy. It's been years since I've used it. I had to rest the back of it against my shoulder. One shot one kill. I'm going to light these motherfuckas up. I swear they're going to regret running up in our home. Thank God I didn't have Shalani with me.

"Young nigga it ain't no bitch or no pussy in me. You better make sure your first move is your best fuckin' move, because if I make it out of this bitch alive. I'll wipe out your whole fuckin' blood line, and that's a fuckin' promise. I'm starting with your momma and your old ass grandmama first." He argued. They got Shon fucked up. He didn't give a fuck about dying but I needed him to fight for us. The way our room was setup. Shon was tied up to a chair. They pistol whipped my baby. He looked at me and smiled. Blood was running down his face.

The robbers had their backs turned. They couldn't see me. They were too busy looking for whatever they could find. Shon nodded his head to the right, he was advising me to take the first shot at the robber on the left. I did as I was told. One shot to the fuckin' head. The boom sounded so loud. The 12 gauge was jumping out of my hand. I had to get a good grip on it.

The second robber looked back and grabbed his gun. He was too slow for me because the 12 gauge was already cocked back, and the bullet had left the chamber already. I hit him dead in the chest. The 12 gauge was a big gun. My shoulder would be hurting for a few days because of the hard impact. I'll take the pain in order to keep Shon alive. I ran to Shon and untied him. He stood up and wrapped his arms around my waist. He was holding me so tight. I don't want him to ever let me go. I broke down crying in his arms. I love him so much. I didn't want to lose him because I almost did.

"Are you okay Shon? I love you. I thought I was about to lose you. I'm sorry for being selfish and only thinking about myself." I cried. I couldn't stop the tears from falling. This is the third time this year, his life has been on the line and I feel bad because I'm the cause of it.

"Stop crying Layla, I'm good. I love you too. I'm straight. I'm not going anywhere. It's not my time yet. Thank you for always coming through for me even when I don't deserve it. You're my guardian angel. You're always on time. Where would I be without you Layla? I don't even want to know." He explained. I ran to the bathroom and got a warm towel to clean Shon's face off. I took my shirt off because I was covered in his blood. Shon was looking at me very intensely.

"Layla, I'm good let's stop for a minute. We need to clean these bodies up." He explained. I wouldn't dare call the police over here to assist us to pick up these stupid ass motherfuckas. I haven't cleaned up a body with Shon in years. We dragged these stupid ass motherfuckas to the basement. I grabbed the AX and Shon cut on the boiler fire place. I chopped the bodies down as small as I could. Shon picked them up and placed them in the fire place.

I walked upstairs to take a shower. I had to pick up Shalani because it was getting late. I didn't have any plans to do this. You'll always have to be prepared for unforeseen circumstances or situations.

Our room was a mess. I cut the shower on to my liking. As soon as I stepped in the tears escaped my eyes. I almost lost him. What if I wouldn't have come home? Shon would've been dead, and I would've never forgiven myself. Shalani would've been without her father. I heard the glass door to the shower open. I looked over my shoulder and it was Shon. A small smile crept up on my face. Even with a few bruises on his face, he was still fine. Shon walked up behind me and backed me into the base of the shower. I gazed into his eyes. He had a small speck of blood on his left cheek. I wiped it off with my hand.

"You couldn't wait on me to take a shower, Layla?" He asked.

"I didn't know if you were coming or not? You were making a few phone calls, so I didn't want to interrupt you. Your mother has Shalani, so I have to pick her up."

"My mother is going to keep Shalani tonight, so it's just you and me. You're not going anywhere. It ain't no breaking up. It's time to make up." "Make up?" I beamed and bit my bottom lip.

"Yeah, we're making up tonight." Shon grabbed my loofa and lathered it with my Dove Amber Rose body soap. He washed my body from head to toe. Shon stopped at pussy and grabbed it.

"You know this belongs to me, Layla? Why the fuck is you trying to take it away from me?" He chuckled. Shon was so full of shit. He continued to wash my stomach and breasts. Shon knew what the fuck he was doing. He was teasing me, and I don't appreciate that shit at all. His touches feel so good.

"I'm not trying to take anything from you. I'm keeping it on reserve until you act right. Come on Shon, let me clean you up, so we can get out of here before the water turns cold."

I washed Shon up and as soon as we got finished the water turned cold. I knew it would because he was too busy trying to fool around. Shon stepped out before I did. He dried off first and wrapped the towel around his waist. I tried to step out and reach for a towel, so I could dry off too. Shon removed the towel from my hands.

"Get out Layla and let me dry you off." He yelled. I did as I was told. I wasn't trying to argue with Shon. We've been through enough today. Shon dried me off and carried me to our guest room. His eyes were trained on me the whole time. I knew he was up to something, but I didn't know what.

"Sit here for a minute Layla, I have to run and get a few things. Don't leave."

"I'm not going anywhere, Shon." I grabbed the remote off the night stand and I threw the oversized comforter over my body. Shon finally made his way back into the room. He approached my side of the bed. He picked me up and laid me on his chest. We both got comfortable. I was listening to Shon's heartbeat.

"Raise up Layla, I need to speak with you for a minute." He stated. He cupped my chin with his free hand, and I stared Shon in his eyes to see what he wanted. His gaze was very intense. He grabbed my hands and he started massaging the two of them.

"Layla you know I love you right?" He asked.

"Yes, what are you trying to say, Shon?" I asked. He's talking in circles. Get to the point.

"Do you want to be with me or you're still threatening to leave me?" He asked.

"Come on Shon, you know I want to be with you. I know I said some shit yesterday that I didn't mean to say. I was mad. I can't take it back, but I do apologize."

"I know Layla and I appreciate that. I always want you to speak about how you feel. Everything you said it needed to be said. I needed to hear that. I respect your feelings and I don't want to ever take them for granted. I should've married you years ago, and you have every right to feel how you feel. I got to come correct that's the only way I'm coming. I don't like how the thought of losing of you feels. I don't want that. I ain't trying to lose you, Layla. I'm ready. Will you marry me? I'm ready to start planning our wedding? I want this. I want us" Shon pulled out a new ring and dangled it in front of me. I snatched it out of his hand and he snatched it back from me.

"Answer my question, I'm waiting." He chuckled. He was smiling. He just knew I was about to say yes. I couldn't even hold my smile in.

"Yes, Shon. I'll marry you. When and where I'll be there." I answered and beamed.

"We have to plan the when and where Layla. I want us to do pre-martial counseling also."

"I'm open to that." I beamed. Shon and I made up. This might be the real thing. I am praying so because I'm ready.

Chapter 22

Malone

It's almost Christmas and it's one of my favorite seasons. I had a lot to be thankful for. Everything is finally falling into place for me and everyone around me. Leah, Layla and I have been talking about getting some Christmas pictures made. We found a photographer who could come out to the house and shoot us. Everybody was here. Leah and Vell, Layla and Shon. It's a family affair we're going to do a group photo also. The only person missing was Lateef, Sphinx's oldest soon. The photographer was already here. Sphinx and I decided to go last because we were waiting for him to come. The photographer has been here for two hours already and Lateef hasn't shown up. I noticed Sphinx in the corner away from everybody. I decided to go over there and see what's going on?

"What's wrong with you?" I asked and cupped his face. I could tell he was about to spaz any minute. He grabbed my hand and led me to our bedroom. Whatever was bothering him he didn't want anybody else to know. He took a seat on our bed and sat me on his lap.

"Everything. Denise isn't bringing Lateef to take the pictures with us. Malone, I swear it's taking everything in me not to go over there and murder her ass. I do every fuckin' thing for him. It's not that easy to cut him off because I've been raising him since he was a fuckin' baby. He's my son no matter what the DNA fuckin' says. I've been raising him. I'm real close to saying fuck it. I give up. I'm not about to play these games with her. She'll fuck around and be dead like that nigga for playing with me. She's reaching Malone and I'll fuckin' touch her. She's being petty for no fuckin' reason."

"I'm sick of her ass Sphinx. I'll be back and don't fuckin' come after me. I'm going to pick up Lateef and check her ass if I'm not back in two hours. Meet me at Dekalb County Jail." I argued. Denise got me so fucked up.

She's tried me for the last fuckin' time and guess what, that shit stops today. Either you want Sphinx to be a father to him or not because he ain't fuckin' got too. My husband ain't a convenience for no fuckin' body but me.

"No Malone, I don't want you going because you can't behave yourself."

"Sphinx I told you to let me handle it months ago, but you didn't. It's a new fuckin' day today. I'm going. Layla and Leah are riding with me."

"I shouldn't have said nothing because you're hard headed as fuck," he argued.

"You didn't have to say anything your face said it all. So what Sphinx, you don't fuckin' listen?" I argued. Sphinx tried to block me from getting up.

"Calm down Malone we're going to take our pictures and then you can go." He argued.

"Okay." Sphinx and I went back downstairs to join the rest of the family and take our pictures. He knew I was in my feelings. Sphinx is a great father. He does more for Jah and Kennedy than Crim ever has. I hate to say it, but it's true. It blows me that Denise would even pull a stunt like this. She knows Sphinx won't cut her water off, but all that shit stops today. It was time for Sphinx and me to take our individual pictures. Every time I looked at him. I had to smile because he was so fuckin' fine. His dreads were freshly twisted, and he was dripping in Gucci. He pulled me into his arms and I bit my bottom lip.

"What are you smiling about?" He asked. Sphinx wanted to know everything. He knew he was the reason for my smile. He just wanted me to admit it.

"Why nosey?" Damn, he can't even let me have my moment. We finished taking our pictures. I really wanted Lateef to be a part of them. I tapped Leah and Layla on their shoulder.

"Come on, I want y'all to ride with me. I got to handle some business and just in case I go to jail. I need somebody to drive my Bentley back home.

"What's going on?" she asked.

"Layla I'll give you the run down in the car." Layla and Leah both grabbed their purses. Leah was snacking on a sweetish meatball and she ran to the bathroom suddenly. Layla and I ran right behind her to see what was up. I could hear her throwing up. Vell pushed us out the way to see what was up with her. He grabbed her hair to avoid throw up getting in it.

"Malone, what the fuck did you put in those meatballs? You got my wife sick!" He yelled and argued. I swear Vell better watch his fuckin' tone. He can't talk to me any kind of way.

"Vell don't go there. I didn't give her anything. It's what you've been giving her. DICK! She's pregnant. Get your silly ass out my face." I argued. Vell looked at me and Layla. Leah cracked a faint smile. I politely moved out the way and reached in the hallway closet and gave Vell a pregnancy test. They closed the door and Layla and I stood outside the door.

"So, do you think Leah is pregnant?" She asked and laughed.

"Oh, I know it. I've been knowing her since I was four. I hate to blow up her spot, but my meatballs are her favorite that's why I made them for her. Did you see your brother come at me all crazy like I poisoned her or some shit?" I laughed. Vell was crazy as hell. The bathroom door opened.

"Malone you don't have to talk about me behind my back." She argued.

"Leah I wasn't talking about you behind your back. I wanted you and Vell to hear me. Are we having a baby or not?" I asked. I'm not about to play with Leah today.

"Yes, we are." She argued and gave me a faint smile.

"I knew it, congratulations. Finally, I'm about to be a godmother. Let's roll." Finally, we were able to leave the house. I grabbed Leah some water, a Ziplock bag, and some crackers.

"What is this for Malone?" She asked.

"In case you get sick again. I don't need you throwing up in my shit." I laughed. I'm just keeping it real.

"Be quiet for a minute y'all let me make this phone call." I dialed Denise's number. I wanted to see where she was at. She answered on the first ring.

"Hey, Denise. We're waiting on Lateef, so we can take the pictures. Are you guys on the way?" I asked.

"Yeah, I'm leaving the nail shop. I'm finna pull up in about thirty minutes. I'm about to leave," she lied.

"Okay cool, where's Lateef? I can pick him up or send him and Uber." I asked. I was pulling this bitches hoe card today.

"He's with me. I'll bring him."

"Okay cool, I'll see you in a few."

"What the fuck is going on?" Layla asked. I gave Layla and Leah the rundown.

"Malone, you need to NIKE check the fuck out of her ass," Leah stated.

"Oh, I plan to. That's why I wanted y'all to ride with me. What nail shop does she go too?"

"Nail Trap on Wesley Chapel." We finished talking and catching up because we haven't done that all week. We were scheduled to get fitted for Layla's wedding next week and now we're about to be planning a baby shower for Leah.

I pulled up at The Nail Trap. Layla and Leah hopped out right behind me. Denise's car was parked up front. I felt the hood. It was cold which means she's been here for a minute. As soon as we walked in all eyes were on us. I locked eyes with Mignon and gave her the smug face. I was looking for Denise. I found her at the pedicure station. I walked right over to her.

"Denise, I need to speak with you?" I argued.

"What's up, Malone?" She argued.

"I need you to pipe the fuck down. You know why I'm here. Let me make some shit clear. Whatever little games you got going on, you can put that shit to a halt. My husband is an amazing father, and nobody can take that from him. Before I came into the picture it wasn't a problem between you and him. It won't be a problem now. You can either get on board or you can get your water cut all the way off. It doesn't make a fuckin' difference to me. It's not him you're hurting, it's your child. What's the fuckin' problem?"

"I don't have a problem, Malone. I had to get somethings situated. I was bringing him." She argued.

"You do have a problem, Denise. It's been going for a few a month's now. I haven't said anything because he asked me not too, but it's a new fuckin' day TODAY. I'm not keeping my mouth shut. You could've handled your business, nobody's stopping you from doing that. We made plans to get family pictures taken today. The only thing you had to do was drop him off or we could've picked him up.

Whatever you had to do you, could've done it. Whatever you and my husband had going on prior to me ain't got shit to do with me or your son, but I feel like you were being spiteful, and I can't stand a spiteful ass bitch. You can never rain on our parade because we will move on with or without you. You ain't stopping shit. You don't have a reason to be spiteful, but if you want to take it there Mr. Baptiste and I can be on our grinch shit. Think about that when you decide to play another fuckin' game." I argued. I didn't have anything else to say.

Everybody was looking at us. I don't give a fuck. I don't know if she thought I was a punk bitch or what but guess what she found out today. Stop playing these games, before I tell Sphinx to say fuck it and not do shit for him. I would never do that because he's been in his life before me and I know how he feels about him. We walked out of the nail shop. Mignon stopped Leah on our way out.

"Leah can I talk to you for a minute," she asked? Layla and I looked at Leah.

"I'm good you know there's not an issue. Pull up front." She argued. Layla stayed inside with Leah. Before I could even get in the car good. My phone went off. I had a text from Sphinx telling me to

Trap God - Pick up Lateef and bring your ass home NOW.

I just read the text I didn't even respond.

Leah

Thank God Vell didn't have any baby momma's because Malone stays chin checking these hoes. What the fuck did Mignon want to talk about? I'm in a real good place right now. Vell and I are expecting but if a bitch got an issue that needs to be addressed, I will lower my standards to check a bitch. I'm not even mad at Mignon. She was cool, but she wasn't Malone, my best friend, and my fuckin' sister. I shouldn't have kept company with her. You live, and you learn. She didn't know any of my secrets, but I knew all of hers.

"What's up?" I asked. I had my arms folded across my chest. Layla was sitting in the chair ready in case a bitch got ignorant. Malone pulled back up in the front of Nail Trap and hopped out. She posted up right by Leah and threw her Gucci bag on the seat next to her. I'm loving the new Malone. I swear she acts just like Leilani.

"Is it okay to talk in front of them, Leah?" She asked.

"Whatever you need to say to me, you can say it in from of them. They're my family."

"Leah, I know I'm probably the last person you want to hear from, but I wanted to apologize. You were a good friend to me. Vell and I messed around before you. I didn't think the relationship was serious because he never committed to anyone since I've known him." Did this bitch just say this? She didn't think it was serious? I had to count to ten before I said what I needed to say. Malone and Layla both stood up.

"Mignon what's understood doesn't need to be explained. You can keep your apology. I guess you want to put on in front of these bitches in here. You know I'll put on a fuckin' show. I'm going to address you one time and one time only. Real bitches do real things. We were cool, but you were never my friend. You knew Vell and I were serious. You came to my engagement party. Out of all the bitches Vell fucked while he was fucking with you, you knew I was that bitch. I had everything to validate that.

A bitch always wants something that they can't have. You kept fucking him because you wanted too. You thought it was cool to smile in my face and fuck him, but you see how that worked out for you. It's a lot of bitches out here that fucked Vell. I'm not them other bitches. I'm

Leah Baptiste, can't no bitch out here validate that. I'm engaged and about to marry him, can't no bitch stake claim to that but me. I'm pregnant with his first child, can't no bitch ever claim that. Mignon, you've always had facts, bitch DON'T ACT. Are we done here, or do I need to state some more FACTS?" I argued. Mignon didn't say another fuckin' word. Bitch don't play with me. We walked out of Nail Trap the same way we came in, harder than motherfucka. I haven't checked a bitch in a long time. Malone pulled off and Layla cut the music off.

"Leah and Malone, what the fuck am I going to do with the two of you? Sphinx and Vell done fucked up big time. Leah, I always knew you were with the shit, but baby you read that bitch like a good book. Malone, you checked Denise and she needed to be checked. I'm proud as fuck to have the two of you as my sisters. I wouldn't have it any other way." She beamed and laughed.

"Layla, I'm glad to have you as a sister too. She tried me. That's the only reason why I turned the fuck up. She saw me plenty of times and didn't say shit, but she wanted to say something to day. I had to give it to her raw." I argued.

"Yes, she tried it, but she wasn't expecting you to clown her silly ass. I saw how those bitches were looking at you, that's why I stayed behind. They weren't expecting you to have the last laugh. The smirks quickly turned into frowns. I'm proud of you Leah because the last time you beat her fuckin' ass. You killed her with kindness this time." She explained. I love Layla to death. I'm glad our circle is so small. No new friends. Malone picked up Lateef and we were headed back to the house. Vell has called me twenty times already telling me to bring his baby back. I'm only two hours pregnant and he's acting a fool.

Chapter 23

Layla

Tomorrow is my wedding day. I'm so ready to say I do. My bachelorette party was last weekend and tonight Dino, Vell, and Sphinx are throwing Shon a bachelors party. Tonight, the girls and I are posted up at The Westin Hotel counting down the hours until Layla and Shon say I do. My mother and Judah have Shalani. I do want one more child, a boy and I'm done after that. Shon hasn't sent me a text, so he must be having fun. Malone and Leah walked in the room fully dressed, with their hands on their hips. Where are they going? Did I miss the fuckin' memo? Trecie and Tati were dressed too.

"Where are y'all going?" I asked. Baby, Malone, and Leah were dressed as if they were going to the club. Malone decided to speak up first.

"Layla, I'm going to Shon's bachelor's party. Yes, we had our little fun last week at your bachelorette party for less than an hour. It's not going down like that. My brother and my husband ruined that shit. If you think for one minute that I'm about to let them niggas shine without any interruptions, you're a gawd damn fool. Go get dressed because we're pulling up at Onyx. I reserved us a VIP Section already," she explained. Malone is crazy as hell.

"Are you serious Malone? You don't trust Sphinx? I trust Shon." I asked.

"I trust Sphinx. I just don't trust these bitches out here. If you would've seen how my husband looked when he left the fuckin' house. Whatever Layla I'm not explaining myself. I'm the only bitch that's going to sit on that dick in any fuckin' club. I don't give two fucks if it's Shon's bachelor party or not. You can babysit the couch if you want, but we're about to pull up." She explained. Leah decided to cut in also.

"I agree with Malone on this one Layla. Why do we have to sit at home and let them have all the fun? If I recall I didn't even get the chance to dance. Your bachelor party was more of a couple's night if you ask me. Let's pull up on those niggas because they would never expect us to pull up." She laughed.

"Damn my bachelorette party was that lame?" I asked and laughed. I swear these bitches ain't shit. They could've told me my party was lame. I didn't mind Shon being there. I wanted to be up under him anyway. I'm the one that gave him the location.

"Yes, because you didn't even get to dance or flirt with another man for the last time. Shon's selfish ass wasn't having that. Remember those guys were going to buy us some drinks, shit as soon as they saw Shon, Sphinx, and Vell it was a wrap. Shit, I can't drink but damn I would've taken a few shots of water just to have fun." She laughed. Tati and Trecie nodded their head in agreeance.

"Okay, Shon is going to be mad as fuck. Yeah, we can pull up. I don't have anything to wear." They think they're slick they had this shit planned already. Sphinx and Vell are going to kill Malone and Leah for their attire.

"Girl whose worried about Shon? I'm not. I have you something cute and slutty picked out. I wouldn't dare step in Onyx without all eyes being on me. He should've thought about that when he decided to pull up. It's not like you weren't coming back home to him. I know Sphinx is having fun because that nigga ain't sent me a text one time.

I sent him a text about an hour ago. I told him I loved him, and he didn't respond." She laughed. Malone and Leah sat a duffel bag on the bed. They pulled out a black leather skirt with fish nets. I swear this skirt was short as fuck. If I decided to bend over everything would be hanging out. I had a white blouse and some peep toe booties.

"Malone and Leah, are trying to get me killed? Because if I bend this ass over it's all coming out. Shon is crazy. I'm not trying to pull a stunt like the two of you." I argued. I already know Shon is about to trip.

"So, what, Layla he's not going to do shit. I want you to bend over. The same way he was loving up on you at your bachelorette party do him the same way. I need you to loosen up and have some fun. If you're scared stay here and we'll see you tomorrow." She argued.

"Malone you ain't nothing but trouble. I do want to see my husband before I go to bed. Sphinx and Vell are going to die. How close is our section to theirs?" I asked.

"Malone Trouble Baptiste, that'll be me. Our VIP is right beside theirs. I just want to see how comfortable they'll be getting a lap dance if we're a few feet away. I'm not having it. Sphinx knows I'm crazy. He doesn't want

another man in my face and I don't want a bitch near him."
She explained. I finished getting dressed. Leah and Malone
hired a driver to chauffer us. They planned this. I took a
shot of Patron. I knew Shon was about to cut up.

Shon

Tonight is my last night as an eligible bachelor. I'm about to do this shit. I'm finally about to marry the love of my life. I can't wait to marry Layla and see the smile on her face tomorrow. Dino, Vell, and Sphinx decided to throw me a bachelors party tonight. I really didn't even want one, but hey this is my last night as a single man. So, I decided to roll with the punches. I'm always on my best behavior. Layla called herself having a little bachelorette party last weekend. I crashed that shit. I didn't want any niggas up in my wife's face.

It's not a woman alive that can compare to Layla. Our VIP section was flooded with hoes and bottles. Damn, I wish my nigga Twin was here. I didn't even feel right because my nigga wasn't here. This was our spot-on Sunday nights. Onyx had some of the baddest bitches I ever saw. The strip club used to be my thing back in the day, but since Layla and I've been back together they haven't seen much of me.

I'm coming of age and my family is the only thing that matters to me. I can't move like that anymore and I didn't want too. It was this bad ass stripper she kept walking past me trying to get my attention. I acknowledged her. I was laid back in my chair rolling my blunt and she came back threw and stopped in front of me.

"Hey, you, I heard tonight was your last night as a single man. Can I dance for you daddy," she cooed and purred like a sex kitten? I don't even want a bitch that close to me let alone dancing up on me. I got too much shit to lose that's why I wasn't drinking.

"I'm good." She licked her lips and gave me a little nasty smirk. I knew she was up to something.

"It's too bad baby, they've already paid me to dance for you. I'll have to do my job and can't waste their money. Would you like a drink to relax you?" she asked.

"Oh yeah?" I asked. She placed her hands on my shoulder and wrapped her hands around my neck. She started grinding on me as her life depended on it. She stood up, turned around and started making her ass shake. Vell, Sphinx, and Dino were making it rain.

Layla

We finally made it to Onyx. They had a nice crowd tonight. Before we made it to our VIP Section, we stopped by the bar because I needed a shot. Leah needed some water and Malone needed some wine. Tati and Trecie ordered four shots of Hennessy. I knew it was about to go down. The waiter came back with all our drinks. I took my shot to the head. It was on. We started strutting through the club on our way to our VIP Section.

Shon's VIP was flooded with bitches and bottles. Yep, it's time to break all that shit up. The smell of weed hit my nose instantly. I saw Sphinx and Vell. Malone and Leah ran to the VIP so Sphinx and Vell wouldn't see them. They were talking all that shit. I was looking for Shon, but I didn't see him. Where the fuck was Shon at? Fuck that, I'm about to walk over there and see what's going on. Malone and Leah grabbed my arm. I jerked my arm back to see what was up?

"Where are you going Layla," Malone and Leah asked.

"To find my motherfuckin' husband," I argued. I know they could tell I had an attitude, but I don't give a fuck. They wanted to pop off, so let's make our presence known. I didn't come here to babysit the VIP Section. I came to make some motherfuckin' noise.

"Okay, that's what the fuck I'm talking about. Let's make our fuckin' presence known them niggas are having a fuckin' ball. Let's stop all that shit." Leah stated. We slapped hands and headed over there. We made it to the VIP section and Vell and Sphinx looked like they saw a ghost. It was a few bitches smiling all up in their face. I still didn't see Shon and I finally found him. It was a stripper popping her pussy all up on him. I locked eyes with Dino and he locked eyes with me and dropped his head.

I know she was just dancing, doing her job, but she was trying to fuck. I saw the lust all in her face. Dino tried to tap Shon. I removed his hand. I snatched that bitch by her long ass weave. I wrapped her hair around in my hand. I had a tight ass grip on her shit. It was a table right beside where Shon was sitting. I rammed her head into the table four fuckin' times. I didn't ease up until I saw fuckin' blood.

Shon had to pull me up off her. Her stripper friends ran over here.

Leah, Malone, Trecie, and Tati were tossing them hoes to the floor. I wish a bitch would touch me. Shon picked me up and carried me out.

"Layla calm the fuck down and bring your motherfuckin' ass on before they call the fuckin' police." He argued. I looked at Shon like he was crazy. I don't give a fuck who they call. They can call Baptiste and son's funeral home for all I care. Better yet I got them on fuckin' stand by.

"Shon, I don't give a fuck about none of that shit, that bitch was too fuckin' close. I'm territorial as fuck and that bitch was trying to get a nut. Let's go. You don't even know how to fuckin' act." I argued and smacked him in the back of his head. "Thank you, Malone and Leah, for bringing me here." Yeah, I had to tell on they ass too. Malone and Leah both cut their eyes at me. Shon carried me outside to his car. He wrapped his arms around me in a bear hug.

"Layla, why are you tripping? It was just a dance." He explained.

"I don't care what it was. I don't play that shit. You know better bitches have ulterior motives." I argued.

"Layla, I didn't even drink shit. My dick ain't even hard, this big motherfucka only gets up for you." He explained. Yeah, that better be true.

"I hear you, take me to my suite and I'll see you tomorrow," I argued. I should've kept my ass in the hotel. Malone and Leah baited the fuck out of me. I had fun though shutting his shit down. Shon knows I'm crazy.

"Fuck that, you're going to ride this dick before I take you to the suite." He argued.

"Whatever Shon." I'm not about to go back and forth with him.

"You heard what the fuck I said, Layla."

Sphinx

Malone Sophia Baptiste got me so fucked up. I don't know what the fuck she's trying to pull. It was her idea to bring Layla here and act a damn fool. She had the nerve to come to the club with that little bitty ass shit on. I swear she wants me to fuck her ass up. She shows her ass just because she knows I won't do shit. She knew I wouldn't approve of her coming out of the house like this. I took my shirt off to cover her ass up. I couldn't wait to get to the car. I got something for her ass. As soon as we made it to the car, I sat her on the hood. I was all up in her personal space. She knew she was in trouble that's why she wouldn't look at me.

"You got something you want to say? I'm trying to see why you have this tight ass dress on showing what belongs to me?" I argued and asked.

"I want you to move out my way and you can put me down Sphinx," she argued. I'm not trying to hear that shit. I put her down and she folded her arms across her chest. My hand roamed her exposed thigh. She tried to swat my hands away. I don't give a fuck about her being mad. She knew better. She tried to snatch the keys out of my hand. I backed her into the trunk of the car. She gazed in my eyes. I gave her a death stare.

"What the fuck are you trying to prove Malone? You know better. You thought it was a good idea to bring Layla here? What if they would've called the police and she would've gone to jail?" I asked and argued. She refused to look at me. I cupped her chin. I was all up in her face. Our lips were touching each other. "Answer my question?"

"Whatever Sphinx. Back up, she didn't go to jail. Y'all ruined our bachelorette party so we crashed y'all shit. We're even. I don't want to talk about it. Take me to the hotel and I'll see you tomorrow You better be glad I didn't bust the bitch who was smiling in your face ass. Save another hoe and see what the fuck happens. Since we pointing out shit, why you didn't text me back? You were having fun, and too busy to text your wife? You got me fucked up. I ain't sorry about shit we did."

"Don't ever tell me to back up. I need you to lose your fuckin' attitude. Malone, why are you tripping on me so hard? I didn't text you back because my phone is almost fuckin' dead. I didn't want my phone to die. You know I love you, why are you questioning that? A bitch can't do shit for me because you do it all. I'm always explaining myself to you.

I got too much to lose to entertain any bitch out here. Baby, you ain't worth losing. I didn't eat shit or drink shit since I've been here. I didn't even get a lap dance. We got Shon a lap dance. Somebody had to take one for the team. Since you came and got me can I take you home? I want to eat and drink you." I asked. Malone had a devilish grin on her face. I knew she was up to no good.

"Nope, I'm going back to the suite with the girls. I'll see you tomorrow and just maybe we can do that." She argued and sassed.

"Is that what you think? We're going home because you don't know how to act. I'm too easy on you. You're taking my kindness as my weakness because I love you. I noticed you like playing on that shit. It's time for daddy to lay down the law. I got something for you. It's time for daddy to be hard on you." I unlocked the door. "Get your ass in the back seat," I argued.

"Why?" She asked. Malone is hard headed as fuck. I pushed her in the back seat. I lifted her dress up and slide her panties down.

"Move Sphinx." She pouted.

"I'm not going anywhere. I asked you could I take you home to eat and drink you? You said no. So, I'm going to get it in right here and then I'll take your hard-headed ass back to the suite. Don't call my phone after I drop you off either. I know why you came here. You wanted this." Malone was wet as fuck It didn't take me no time to make myself at home. It didn't take her no time to start grinding on this dick. As soon as she got comfortable and I felt she was about nut. I pulled out and pulled my pants back up. Two can play that game.

"Put it back in," she argued and moaned. I wanted to laugh in her face so bad.

"Nope, I'm tired of you using me for my dick. You wanted to go to the suite so bad, so that's where I'm taking you. I'll see you tomorrow, hopefully, you'll be on your best behavior.

EPILOGUE

MARCH 8,2019

Chapter 24

Layla

I'm so nervous and I shouldn't be. My palms were sweaty. I had to wipe my hands with a paper towel. Everything that I wanted is finally about to happen. Who would've known Shon is finally about to marry little old me. It's crazy because I've been wanting him to marry me forever. This is the final storm that I thought we wouldn't be able to weather. I counted Shon out and doubted him for the longest. I shouldn't have because he's always made things happen for us. In a matter of minutes, I'll be Layla Renee Adams officially. Shon and I have so much history this is the only thing that hasn't been written. I'm ready to make a few new memories. It's finally about to happen and I'm going to die of shock before it happens. Please let me make it to the alter in one piece.

I've been waiting on this day for months. I haven't seen Shon in over twenty-four hours and that's a first for us, in a matter of months. I can't believe we're about to do this. I guess its true good things come to those who wait. Lord knows I've been waiting for forever. Throughout this journey or ride we've been on, I didn't have patience. I lacked patience. Patience is the virtue and the key to happiness. I was worrying and praying so much, and I shouldn't have been worrying because I knew God wouldn't bring me this far again just to upset me. It was a test and I almost failed.

The moment Malone and Sphinx said I do I wanted that too. The moment Malone had her twins I wanted my daughter to come too. Every lesson has a blessing and I've learned a few. When it's your time, nobody can take that from you. Nothing happens when you want it to, but it's always right on time.

"Layla, it's almost time are you ready?" My mother and Leilani asked.

"Of course, I am." I beamed. I was having hot flashes. I used a church fain to cool me off. I had to get myself together quick. Giselle did my hair and make-up. Our colors were lavender and white. My dress was lavender and draped in diamonds. Shon's tux was white with a small hint of lavender. I couldn't wait to see how he looked in his fitted tux. Tati and Trecie were my both my matrons of honor. Malone was my maid of honor. Leah was a bridesmaid. Vell was walking me down the aisle. I looked in the mirror to make sure my make-up was on point. Giselle beat my face to the gawds.

"Layla Renee Adams." I looked over my shoulder to see what my mommy wanted.

"Yes, mommy?" I asked.

"Baby girl why are you so nervous? Sit down for a minute." I did as I was told. My mother grabbed the fan and started fanning me. "I've never seen you this nervous a day in your life. Everything that has gone wrong with you and Shon has already happened. Everything you went through was for you to reach this point. I speak life over your union. I wish you two nothing but the best. I know you better than you know yourself.

One thing that you're sure of is how much Shon loves you. Your nerves should never be a wreck baby girl. You're perfect and Shon loves you just the way you are. I'm so happy that I'm alive and able to witness this because I know how much you've wanted this. Marrying him should be natural for you. I have something that I want to give you. It's my mother's necklace she gave me this when I married your father. I want you to have it too." My mother placed the necklace around my neck.

"Thank you, mommy, I appreciate, you." Vell came in the room and interrupted our moment. It's time to get this show on the road.

"Layla let's go its time. We're waiting for you." He asked. Vell grabbed my hand and escorted me out.

Shon

Layla and I have been planning this wedding for months. I swear I wanted this day to be perfect for her. My nerves are bad as fuck. She almost gave up on us. Today was all about her and our union. She deserves nothing but the best, for putting up with me for all these years. I know it hasn't been easy, but we finally made it here. I'm nervous as fuck. What if she doesn't show up? I know God didn't bring me this far to be down on my luck. I wish my nigga was here, but I know he's here in spirit. I had an empty chair and a portrait of him that sat in the chair. I don't care if Sphinx wasn't feeling it. Twin was my nigga until the casket dropped. I wasn't getting married if my partner in crime wasn't near. Long Live Twin. I live by and die by that shit. I'll rep him until the death of me.

Dino was my best man. Sphinx and Vell were my groomsmen. Layla looked so beautiful walking down the aisle. I couldn't stop looking at her. She finally approached me. We're finally about to do this. I'm ready. It's been a long time coming. As soon as she made it to me. I took both of her hands into mine. I let Juan start our service. My mother, OG Lou and my Auntie Linda Faye were on the front row. My daughter was cutting up and putting on a show. I guess she wanted us to get her.

"We're gathered here today to witness the union of Layla Baptiste and Shon Adams. I'm honored to officiate over their union. I've been knowing Shon and Layla forever. We grew up together. We went to Middle and High school together. I was honored to marry them because I watched them grow. I know them. I've witnessed their highs and their lows. I'm not even surprised that we're here today.

Marriage is a beautiful thing and I'm glad Layla and Shon are finally about to do this. It's been a long time coming and I'm honored to bless their union. I ran into Shon a few months ago in Shane's jeweler. I was upgrading my wife's ring and Shon he was doing a few upgrades too. We stopped and caught up with each other for a minute. He told me he was finally about to marry Layla before she leaves him.

I couldn't believe it because they've been together since High School. I would've thought they would've been married already. I wanted to meet with Shon and Layla before they got married. I wanted to see why they wanted to do it?

Black love is beautiful. Besides how they portray us in the media. Black men love our Black queens. Marriage, it's a lot of work. On the outside looking in, everybody wants to do it just for the title, wealth, likes on social media, and relationship goals post. Don't do it for anybody else. Do it for yourself. It takes communication and dedication. A lot of people aren't willing to put in the required work that it takes for a marriage.

We had a serious conversation at our pre-marital counseling. I asked Layla why she wanted to marry Shon? Why now? She had a lot to say and I was blown away. It was genuine and real. I've married a lot of people. When Layla spoke about Shon, I could feel it. Her words held so much confidence, love, power, and respect. I could tell this was the real thing. Layla, I want you to share with us a few of your thoughts from our conversation."

"Oh, my where do I begin? I'm about to mess up my make-up because once I get started these tears will never end. I've loved Shon my whole life. I've been fighting for this moment for ever and a day. Today we're finally about to get it right. I've been waiting for this day since I was sixteen. I knew he was meant for me then. I dreamt of this for so long and it's finally about to happen. I wrote my vows to him over ten years ago. It's cliché right.

He was my first and my only love. Our road getting here wasn't pretty when I look back and think about us. Sometimes I trip on how happy we used to be. It's not about how you start it's about how you finish. It's not about the good days, because we've had plenty of those. It's about our bad days that outweighed them all. Somehow, we overcame those. God puts people in your life for a reason and season. Shon and I were apart for years because HE couldn't get it right. WE couldn't get it right.

Sometimes you'll have to leave in order to find your place. I left. I thought I found my place with someone else. God had other plans for us. He placed us in a room with each other and dangled our love over us.

The moment we locked eyes with each other it was a wrap. He invaded my mind and hours later he captured my body and soul.

His love had a hold on me that I could never shake. Even with our history and our undying chemistry, our love could never be erased. Never put a time limit on love. True love can never be replaced. We met back up a year ago today, who knew today our wedding would be taking place? I love you Shon with all my heart and I'm more than ready for our fresh start." She explained. Layla's words were tugging at my heart.

"Shon, I want you to share your feelings from our conversation?" He asked. Bishop Ryan didn't have a problem with putting me on the spot. It's all good. I knelt on one knee. I grabbed Layla's hands because I wanted her to feel me. Dino passed me the crown.

"I really didn't want to do this. I just wanted to say I do. It is what it is. I don't have a problem with letting the world know how I feel about you. Layla Renee Adams. The first time I laid eyes on you. I knew I had to have you. Nothing or no one was going to stop me from getting at you. You've always had me in a trance. The moment I met you, you took my heart from me and never gave it back to me. If I was to die today, I want you to keep that. I've never been in love before until I met you. You're the only woman I ever loved. Besides my mother and sister, and now my daughter. You're the only woman I've told I love you. You're the only one I want to experience it with. You're the only woman besides my daughter that will carry my last name.

Excuse my language but I fucked up a few times when it came to us. I took you for granted more than once. The years we were apart was some of the hardest years of my life. I always wondered why my luck was bad. It was because I didn't treat you right. It's this thing called Karma. She had a hard on for me for years because of how I treated my precious Layla. Our relationship hasn't been perfect, and it was because of me. I'm man enough to own up to all of it. You've always been perfect to me, never doubt that for one minute. It was me, not you. We've had our share of difficulties. Layla, you're my queen and I want you to wear this crown.

You deserve the world and more. I will die giving it to you. We crossed paths again for a reason, baby, it's our season. When I saw you again, I vowed to never let you walk away from me. God made you for me. With you and my daughter is the only place I want to be. You're the air I breathe, promise me you'll never leave or give up on me. I want you to be my wife.

I promise to love you and cherish you for life. It's nothing in this world that I won't do for you. I thank God every day for bringing you back to me. Will you marry me please?" Layla was crying. I had to wipe her tears away. I meant everything I said.

"Shon, do you take Layla Baptiste to be your wife?"

"I do."

"Layla, do you take Shon Adams to be your husband?"

"I do."

"I now pronounce you husband and wife. You may now kiss the bride."

THE END

Pushing Pen Presents now accepting submissions for the following genres: Urban Fiction, Street Lit, Urban Romance, Women's Fiction, BWWM Romance Please submit your first three chapters in a Word document, synopsis, and include contact information via email @pushingpenpresents@gmail.com please allow 3-5 business days for a response after submitting.

Giselle & Vic
Giving My Heart To A Boss

NIKKI NICOLE

YOU DON'T MISS A GOOD THING Until It's Gone

NIKKI NICOLE

CPSIA information can be obtained
at www.ICGtesting.com
Printed in the USA
LVHW011723090119
603318LV00015B/234/P